M000107674

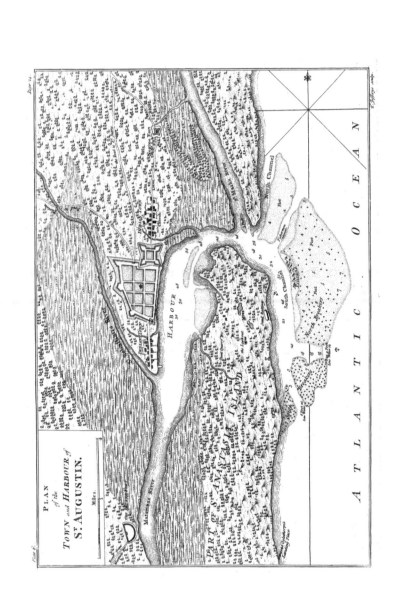

PLAN of the TOWN and HARBOUR of ST. AUGUSTIN.

Miles.

Matanzas River

PART of ANASTASIA ISLAND

HARBOUR of

North Channel

South Channel

Anastasia Island

ATLANTIC OCEAN

Saving Home

Judy Lindquist

PUBLISHER'S NOTE

This novel is a work of fiction. Names, characters, places and incidents either are the product of the author's imagination or are used fictitiously, and any resemblance to actual persons living or dead, events, or locales is entirely coincidental.

Copyright ©2008 by Judy Lindquist

All rights are reserved under International and Pan-American Copyright Conventions. No part of this book may be reproduced in any form or by any means, electronic or mechanical, including photocopying, recording or by any information storage and retrieval system, without permission in writing from the publisher, except by a reviewer who may quote brief passages in a review.

Manufactured in the United States of America
ISBN 1-886104-35-2

Published by
The Florida Historical Society Press
435 Brevard Avenue
Cocoa, Florida 32922
Phone (321) 690-1971
FHSPress@myfloridahistory.org

P•R•E•S•S

This book is dedicated to Jeff, for never letting me give up; to Sarah, for your inspiration; to mom and dad for your unshakable belief; and to my students- you are the shining stars that light the future!

Chapter 1

Luissa de Cueva stopped so abruptly, the scruffy gray dog following at her heels ran into her, nearly knocking her down.

"Look!" she exclaimed as she pointed to the town plaza.

Her friend Diego stuffed a last fistful of berries into his mouth before he stopped in amazement. Swallowing, he whispered, "What do you think is going on?"

Hundreds of townspeople had gathered in the St. Augustine town plaza and the crowd was listening intently to the imposing figure standing on the platform. The colorful sea of faces and clothing reflected the town. Closest to the platform were the Spanish soldiers not on duty in the massive fort that stood at the bay. There were friars and priests peppered throughout the crowd, distinguished by their religious robes. There were also freed slaves, Guale, Timucua and Apalachee Indians who had converted to Christianity, as well as the Spanish citizens who called the garrison home. Judging

1

by the serious look on the faces of those in the crowd, the children knew something important was happening.

Quietly, the two children made their way to the edge of the crowd. Although they seemed to be the only children in the gathering, no one noticed as they inched their way forward toward the platform.

Governor Jose de Zuniga y Cerda stood at the front of the stage addressing the crowd. He was not a tall man, but he carried himself with the authority of a man twice his height. He spoke clearly and with a tone that only a man of great confidence and determination could have.

"We must take this threat seriously," he was saying. "Unfortunately, it may take many days before my requests for help are received and acted upon, so we must plan on defending ourselves without aid from Havana, Pensacola or French Mobile. We are on our own- at least initially."

The crowd stirred as they absorbed what the governor had just said, some nodding in agreement, and others commenting quietly to each other. He assured the townspeople that he would keep them informed and then in an instant, he disappeared from sight.

As the people in the crowd started to disperse, Luissa and Diego looked at each other, puzzled. Neither was sure of exactly what was going on. Luissa's dark eyes reflected her serious nature as she tried to absorb what was just said.

Luissa was tall for a 9-year-old, and even in her long skirts and petticoats, she was quick and agile. Her long dark hair hung in a thick braid down the middle of her back. That braid had many times been pulled in playfulness by her companion, Diego de las Alas.

Although he was a year older, he was no taller than Luissa. The two had been best friends for nearly as long as they could remember. They were an inseparable pair, her seriousness balancing his mischievous playfulness.

Although at this time, his usual lighthearted manner had given way to a pensive look that mirrored Luissa's.

"What are you two doing here?" The loud question interrupted their musings as they turned to face Diego's brother Rodrigo. What Diego lacked in height, his brother seemed to have made up for, as he was exceptionally tall for a 14 year old. "I thought you were gathering berries." His tone was suspicious as he looked down on the two friends.

"We were," said Diego as he and Luissa each held up their baskets to show him the evidence of their work.

"What's happening?" asked Luissa, always one to get right to the point.

"Looks like there is going to be a battle!" said Rodrigo, almost gleefully.

"What do you mean?"

"Against who?"

"Here in St. Augustine?"

"Why?"

The questions fell over each other as the two tried to understand.

Rodrigo took a deep breath and held up his hand. "Wait a minute," he said patiently. Although he sometimes liked to tease his younger brother and his friend, he also felt protective toward them and knew how confusing this situation must seem to them. "Let's see if I can explain it...."

3

"Seems the English troops from Carolina are planning on attacking us-"

"Attack us?!" interrupted Luissa, "Why?"

"Why else? To gain control of the city, the fort, and the bay. This is an important stop on the route of trade ships, you know."

"What are we going to do?" whispered Luissa.

"We don't have to do anything. Our soldiers will protect us. They'll blast those English ships right out of the water as soon as they sail into the harbor," explained Rodrigo with such confidence that both Luissa and Diego believed him.

By the time the children headed for home, the crowd had long since dissipated and the sun was starting to set. As the last streaks of sunlight pierced their way through the large trees, the warm temperatures of the late October afternoon faded into the brisk coolness of night.

The large buildings that surrounded the town plaza soon gave way to more modest wooded structures as the children wandered down St. George Street.

St. Augustine, a Spanish garrison town, was founded in 1565 and in the 137 years since then, had grown in many ways. The town was now not only occupied by the soldiers commissioned to protect the town, but by their families and the many missionaries sent to help spread Christianity. Many of the workers and craftsmen sent to help with the construction of the huge coquina fort had stayed on, and made St. Augustine their home.

The children soon got to the corner of Cuna St. and Luissa's house. Her dog Lobo, who was walking in

4

front of them this time, froze in his steps. The fur on his back stood up and a low growl rumbled from deep down inside of him. His alert eyes narrowed as he locked in on his prey. A second later he was flying through the underbrush in hot pursuit of the poor creature who would be his victim.

"Oh no!" said Rodrigo, "Do we need to go after him?"

"No," explained Luissa, "he's always running off after something. He always comes back on his own. Sometimes right away, sometimes after a day or two. Papa says it's because he is not totally domesticated. He's still got a wild side."

Satisfied that she did not need their help to retrieve her beloved pet, Diego and Rodrigo headed off to their house while Luissa turned down her street.

Arriving home with the last shadows of the day, Luissa set her basket of berries on the large wooded table that dominated one side of the room.

The de Cueva family home was no larger than most of the other homes in St. Augustine. It was a wooden structure with a thatched palm frond roof and was one large room. Because Luissa's father was a carpenter, they did however, have more furniture than many other families. The large metal brasero was in the center of the room, its coals glowing red and giving off waves of heat that slowly warmed the cold room. The table and chairs, plus a storage cabinet were in the back of the house while two ornate storage chests, a plain wooden bed and a wooden cradle were in the front of the room. Luissa's parents slept in the bed and her baby brother Benito, in the cradle. Luissa, like most children her age, unrolled her Spanish moss-stuffed mattress onto the floor each night. In the fall and winter she would place it as close to the brasero as her mother would let her. In the spring and summer she would place it under the eastern window to take advantage of the sea breeze that blew in off the bay.

"Where have you been?" questioned her mother as she reached over and ran her hands through the berries in the basket. "I was getting worried."

"We're going to be attacked!" exclaimed Luissa. "We heard the governor in the town square. Rodrigo says we don't have to worry though, because our soldiers will just blast them- the English- right out of the water." She said very matter-of-factly.

"As simple as that, is it?" asked Luissa's father who had come in the door behind her.

"Isn't it?" asked Luissa, her earlier confidence fading.

"Well," said her father settling down into one of the chairs at the table, "I was at the plaza today too. Unfortunately, it's not as simple as that. We are a military town, but our greatest asset- our only asset it seems- is the Castillo de San Marcos. The fort. Other than that, we are short on trained soldiers, we have little weaponry and artillery, and much of what we have is in need of repair. If the English do attack, it will not be simple. No battle can ever be simple."

Sensing Luissa's growing fear and confusion, her mother stepped in and ended the conversation by asking her to help get dinner set for the family. She gave her husband a knowing look over Luissa's head.

The next day found Luissa helping her father. She was measuring and lining up the pieces of wood that

6

were going to be the legs of a chair he was currently building. His work area was a wooden lean-to, built behind their house. The open structure allowed the breeze to keep his work area cool.

Though the young Spanish girls of the town were traditionally trained by their mothers in all of the ways of homemaking, some also learned their father's trade. While they could not officially be apprenticed, they could work at their father's sides, perfecting their skills.

Luissa had been trailing around after her father since she was old enough to follow directions. By the time she was 6 years old, she knew the names of all the tools and how they worked. By eight she was retrieving tools and wood when he needed them. Now, at 9 years old, she even occasionally used a hand lathe to bore a hole or to plane a smooth rough edge. She loved the idea of taking a plain piece of wood and creating something with it. Watching it go from a rough, jagged plank to a smooth sturdy tabletop or a strong, carved chair.

As the afternoon sun began its descent, Luissa handed her father the last leg to be pegged into the chair. She was starting to sweep up the piles of discarded wood shavings when she caught sight of her wandering dog coming around the corner.

"Lobo!" she cried as she dropped the broom and crouched down so the dog could bound into her arms, knocking her off her feet. She giggled as the big shaggy dog licked her face. No matter how many times he ran off, Luissa always worried until he came back.

Her dog had been a part of the family since he showed up at their door six years ago. He just appeared out of nowhere and three-year-old Luissa had fallen in love with him. The feeling appeared to be mutual, since when he wasn't off chasing rabbits, squirrels and other creatures, he was Luissa's constant companion.

"Well Lobo," said her father, looking at the dog's matted fur and dirty legs, "Looks like you were exploring the marshes again."

Just then Diego came around the side of the house.

"Hello Diego," Luissa said to her friend. "Look, I told you he would come back." She stopped and stood up when she saw the look on her friend's face. Diego's normal, carefree expression was heavy with worry.

"What's the matter?" she questioned.

"The governor put all soldiers on 24-hour alert and they all have to report to the Castillo. My papa just left with his things." Diego looked at his feet as he went on. "You know, he has been on duty in the fort lots of times, sometimes for a week or more without being able to see him. It was always alright. But this time I have a really awful feeling in my stomach."

Luissa's father reached over and put his hand on Diego's shoulder. "I have the same feeling- and it's called fear. Fear is not necessarily a bad thing. It can make us more alert, aware," he said gently.

Diego looked up. "The governor has given orders that no one is to leave the city walls... I think this is pretty serious."

Chapter 2

November third dawned clear and cool. The warm summer weather that sometimes lasted into late fall in Florida had finally been pushed out by the dry, cooler air that marked the winter months. The sky was dotted with an occasional cloud that broke up the expanse of deep blue.

It had been a week since the governor had stood in the town plaza and addressed the townspeople regarding the threat from the north. The first couple of days after that, the town had been abuzz with activity and gossip. It was the focus of everyone's attention and every conversation centered on the possible confrontation. But as the hours and days passed and no further announcements came, the people of St. Augustine had settled back into a fairly normal routine.

All of the soldiers were on duty in the fort, but that was only a portion of the population of the city. There were the wives and children of the military men. There were also the tradesmen who had settled in the town, like Luissa's father, and various converted Indians and freed slaves. Many of these had taken up farming when they settled in St. Augustine.

Although on the surface the town seemed to be going about its daily business as normally as possible, there was a rush of activity at the fort. The governor and his advisors had repeatedly sent out letters explaining the town's dire circumstances and asking for aid. Letters had been dispatched over land and by sea to many of the other Spanish outposts in Florida, as well as to Havana.

After gathering the soldiers in the fort and surveying the artillery, Governor Zuniga realized that their position was even weaker than he had anticipated. However, the people of the town were unaware of just how precarious their safety was.

Now that the days were cooler, Luissa's mother tried to keep the brasero burning most of the day to keep the baby warm, so Luissa had the additional chore of fetching the charcoal and kindling when needed. This morning, after completing her other chores, she set out for the town plaza which also functioned as a market where people went to barter for goods and services.

In the town square Luissa got her bucket filled with coal and was making her way back to St. George Street when she caught sight of another of her friends.

"Junco!" called Luissa, waving to get her friend's attention.

Junco lived at the Mission of Nombre de Dios, which lay just beyond the northern edge of the city. She had come to the mission with her parents when they were converted to Christianity by the Franciscan Missionaries who worked there. She was just a baby then, so she had no memory of life before the mission.

When the Spanish government had decided to set up settlements in the New World, they determined that part of their goal would be to bring the word of God to the natives that lived there. They did this by setting up Missions where they would educate and civilize the tribes that they found. The Indians would live on the mission grounds, where they would receive instruction in the Catholic Religion, as well as the ways of the Spaniards. They would also be expected to work in the fields that the Spanish owned. The Spanish government viewed this as a positive arrangement for everyone. They got the much needed help to plant and harvest their crops and the Indians learned how to farm in the ways of the Spaniards which they felt were better than the ways of the Indians.

There were many missions up and down the coast of Florida and some inland as well. Some missions worked with the Guale Indians, some with the Apalachee and some, like the Mission of Nombre de Dios, with the Timucua tribes.

Junco's family was from the Timucua tribe. She was part of the clan of the Panther, but all she knew of her clan was what her parents and grandparents told her. She was able to speak both her native language and Spanish, although her Spanish was not as fluent. She had grown up in the city of St. Augustine and was about the same age as Luissa. When she wasn't working or studying, she loved to spend time with Luissa and Diego since there were so few children at the mission.

"You have more chores to do?" she asked Luissa when she caught up with her friend.

"I just have to bring this back home and then maybe we can go down to the bay?" Luissa enthusiastically asked. One of their favorite pastimes was to walk along the bay and collect seashells.

The girls spent the rest of the daylight hours doing just that. By the time they parted company both were exhausted and not far from bed.

In her dreams the church bells were ringing. The people of the town were all rushing toward the mission, their voices mixing into a sea of words.

Luissa rolled over and slowly awakened from her dream, realizing that the words were her parents talking somewhere in the blackness of the night and that church bells were indeed ringing. The echoing clang was not the same rhythmic sounds she heard each Sunday. Instead, this ringing had an uneven urgency to it that demanded attention.

Her mother hastily wrapped a shawl around her shoulders as both her parents stepped outside to investigate the commotion. Luissa sat up and rubbed the sleep from her eyes, trying to focus in the darkness.

Adding to the noise of the night, Luissa's baby brother woke and started to wail. Quickly, Luissa got up and picked up three-month-old Benito. She started to slowly bounce him as she cooed to him. "It's alright" she whispered as she followed her parents outside.

In the distance the sky glowed red, yellow and orange above the treetops. The moon was only a sliver in the sky, so offered no illumination in the darkness. From her backyard, the view was blocked by other homes and trees. Luissa stared at the sky trying to figure out what was causing the strange glow.

She slowly became aware of the voices and people in the dark. Shadowy figures were moving east down the street toward the bay and river. Carrying her now quieted brother, Luissa followed the figures in the cold night, so intent that she barely noticed the ice cold dirt beneath her bare feet.

The street ended at the sea wall of the bay and river. Across the expanse of water that was Matanzas Bay, far out of sight to the northeast, laid Amelia Island. The Island was home to the San Luis Mission and a fort. There was also a guardhouse and watchtower. Amelia Island was the first stop for most of the ships coming south into Matanzas Bay and St. Augustine.

Seeing her parents in the crowd, Luissa moved beside them, but so intent were they on the far off island that they didn't even notice her. Her father had put his arm around her mother as they stood rigid in the cold night. The crowd was slowly growing as more people made their way to the edge of the river. Yet even as their numbers multiplied, the eerie quiet was never broken. People simply stared in disbelief.

In the distance, a glow lit the sky. Smoke billowed into the sky, quickly becoming invisible in the darkness of the night. An occasional spire of flames shot up into the sky as if reaching for the heavens as the church bells continued their relentless ringing.

The reality of what they were witnessing slowly grew until someone finally broke the silence.

"The English soldiers have arrived," someone said.

Chapter 3

Luissa and Diego sat in silence on the simple rock wall that marked the edge of Matanzas Bay. Their feet dangled as they peered intently out to sea. The sun was directly above them and shone down with clarity and warmth. It reflected off the shimmering water causing them to squint in the brilliance.

Luissa had wanted to come down to the bay first thing that morning, but her mother would not let her. It was the Sabbath and as always, they would spend it at the St. Francis Monastery and church where they always attended Sunday mass.

Setting off for the monastery that morning with her family, Luissa had held her father's hand extra tightly. Both her parents were quiet, lost in their own thoughts. As they approached the stone monastery, the gray cross and spire rose in the morning sky.

Despite the fact that all of the soldiers were on duty in the fort, the rest of the town filled the chapel for the Sunday service. With last night's events on everyone's mind, prayers were intense and the service almost urgent.

Now, starting across the bay, the children tried to focus their eyes in the direction of Amelia Island. It was impossible to see it in the brightness of day. They had to look beyond Anastasia Island, which was directly across from them. That was close enough for them to see the occasional trees and shrubs growing along its shore. Amelia Island, however, was not visible. There were still light columns of smoke that rose sporadically in the distance, marking its location.

Things seemed strangely quiet after the commotion of the night before. Governor Zuniga had dispatched one of his captains and 20 soldiers to the Island in hopes of foiling the English progress. Given the location of the flames of the night before, it was assumed that some of the important structures on the island were destroyed, but having received no official word yet from those stationed there, the Governor was hoping for the best. The heavy smoke had continued through the night and well into the morning hours.

"We've been sitting here for hours and haven't gotten a peep of an Englishman. Maybe it wasn't them after all," said Diego.

"Of course it was them," said Luissa very matter of factly. "Who else would land on Amelia Island and start to burn things down?"

"Well I just want to get a look at one of them," Diego explained.

"I'm not sure why," said Luissa reflectively, "It's not going to change anything."

"Aren't you even curious?" Diego looked at Luissa in disbelief. "Don't you wonder what they look like?"

"No," she stated firmly. Then added, "Oh, maybe a part of me does want to see what they look like, but another part hopes I never, ever see one of those horrid English soldiers. Maybe they did what they wanted to do and now they are going back to Carolina," she said hopefully.

"Not much chance of that," said Diego as he continued to focus in the direction of the island.

"The island seems a lot farther away in the daylight than it did last night," stated Luissa. "Last night I felt like they were right at our door ready to burst right in. But today, I can't even see the island...it seems so far away."

"Not as far away as you think," said a quiet voice behind from them.

The children turned to see Junco standing behind them, her face as serious as theirs. She sat down beside Luissa, her cloth skirt dangling down to her bare feet.

"Much commotion at the mission," she stated as she joined her friends in gazing in the direction of the invisible island.

"The mission here? Why?" asked Luissa.

"The Timucua are afraid of the English. They destroy other missions to the north. They destroy the mission on the island last night. The Nombre de Dios might be next. The Timucua know if they stay, they could be captured and be slaves. If they run away, perhaps they can find brother tribes and escape battle."

"But all of the Timucua at the mission are converts- Christians-you can't just go back to being like some of the other tribes. You're like us now!" Luissa's voice was pleading.

"Maybe," said Junco, "but maybe we never lose old ways. Sometimes elders talk about old times. When priests not around. Old ways don't sound so bad."

The children sat quietly for awhile, each lost in their own thoughts. Diego finally broke the silence.

"Do you think your family will leave?"

Junco just shrugged her shoulders.

By the time Luissa and Diego said good bye to Junco, the sun was making its descent. They began their walk back to Diego's in silence.

Diego's house was similar to Luissa's in style. Most homes were wood construction with palmetto thatched roofs. Windows on the east and west sides allowed for the sea breeze to blow through. The doors to Spanish homes, however, were not at the front of the structures. Instead, one usually had to go through a side courtyard to find the front door. Diego's house was no different and it was in this small courtyard that the children found Diego's mother.

Senõra de las Alas was a beautiful woman. Her black hair was pulled back into a thick bun and her usually sparkling blue eyes were cloudy and sad. She was sitting on a wooden bench and as Diego approached, he thought he saw signs of tears on her creamy cheeks.

"What is wrong Mama?" he questioned, sitting next to her on the bench.

She took a deep breath. "The Governor has ordered all men- 14-years-old and older- to report to the Castillo to be armed. Rodrigo is gathering his things now."

"What?" Luissa asked, not sure she understood. "You mean Rodrigo has to be a soldier in the fort? What if he doesn't want to?"

"I'm afraid he has no choice," said Diego's mother calmly, patting Luissa's hand and taking Diego's with the other. "The English are nearly here. It is obvious the reports are true and they plan on attacking St. Augustine. We do not have enough commissioned soldiers to defend the city. The governor needs our young men. We all do."

Diego, who was sitting quietly, abruptly jumped up. His eyes were a mixture of anger, confusion and fear. He looked at his mother then at Luissa. Without saying a word, Diego charged into the house, slamming the door behind him.

Luissa started to follow her friend, but Senõra de las Alas put her arm out to stop her.

"He will be alright. I think he just needs some time. Why don't you go home for awhile and perhaps come back this evening. I'm sure he will be better by then. I'm sure you will want to see your papa before he reports to the fort as well."

Luissa looked startled. She had not realized that her papa would be affected as well. All of the men in the city were now soldiers, whether they wanted to be or not. Without a word, she turned and ran home.

Inside the de las Alas house, Rodrigo was quietly gathering up a few pieces of clothing and putting them into his pack. Diego sat down and watched his brother carefully button up his vest.

"So, you get to be a soldier?" he asked hesitantly.

"Seems that way," Rodrigo answered quietly. He finished tying his pack shut and set it on the floor.

"What do you think it will be like? Being a soldier, I mean." Diego was watching his brother's face intently.

"Well, I imagine it will be a little confusing at first. Until I get to know exactly what to do. It will probably be busy. We will have lots to do."

"Do- do you think it will be scary?" asked Diego with trepidation.

Rodrigo stood looking at his younger brother. "Yes. I'm sure it will be scary. But that's alright. Because I know I will be doing something important, protecting our home. You will be doing something important too, Diego. You will need to help out mama. With both papa and me on duty in the fort, she will really need you."

Diego's eyes never left his brother's face. He studied his brother's expression and knew that he was more frightened than he would admit.

"Perhaps you will get to work with papa as an artillery man," said Diego.

"That would be nice," smiled Rodrigo. "Now I've got to go," he said picking up his pack.

Diego hesitated a moment, thinking how the grown up thing to do would be to shake his brother's hand. Instead he threw his arms around his brother's waist, nearly knocking him over.

"Be careful," Diego said, his voice muffled by his brother's clothes and the tears that were filling his throat.

Chapter 4

Luissa tensely leaned over the tub of water and continued to ferociously wash out the pottery bowl, her eyes wandering from the task at hand to the door of their house. Luissa had been flitting about all morning, "like a bumblebee" her mother had said, the tenseness making her jumpy and energetic. She had completed all of her daily chores in less time than normal, but had hardly been focused on what she was doing.

Last night had been another eventful evening for the people of St. Augustine. The sentry in the northeast lookout of the Castillo de San Marcos had spotted three English ships as they sailed into view to the north. While they were still quite far from landfall, warnings had been issued and soldiers readied.

Then, early this morning, word had come that the governor was going to address the townspeople in the city square. Luissa was ready to go charging out the door with her father, who did not have to report to the fort until later that day. However, Senõr de Cueva had insisted that his young daughter stay at home with her mother and baby brother.

Although he had not been gone more than an hour, to Luissa it felt like days and she once more went to the front window to look down the street. When he finally did arrive home, she didn't even have time to utter a single question before her father asked them all to sit down at the table.

Luissa looked across the table at her father's face and thought she would burst if he didn't say something.

"The governor has ordered all of the people of St. Augustine into the fort for protection," he began. Luissa started to open her mouth, but her father held up his hand.

"I know you have a lot of questions, but I want you to let me finish explaining what I know first. I want you to really listen. Then you can ask questions all right?"

Luissa nodded.

Her father's glance went from Luissa to her mother and back again as he started to summarize the governor's orders.

"The governor has received word that the English have captured Santa Maria Island as well as Amelia Island. It seems at this point there is nothing between them and us. They also have forces inland which are traveling south down the Salamoto River. They are approaching by land and sea and we do not have enough men or ammunition to defend the entire city. The governor has once again sent requests for help but since we do not know when it will arrive, the only safe place for everyone is inside the Castillo de San Marcos."

Luissa's father looked to see if she understood.

"Every family is to report to the fort with just their valuables and we are to plan on this being an extended siege."

He waited a moment for both Luissa and her mother to absorb the enormity of what he had just said.

"All of the livestock will be herded into the dry mote and everyone is to turn over all of their food supplies- corn, flour, beans- for safekeeping and for distribution."

The silence stretched on for several minutes before he went on.

"Some of our soldiers are dismantling the planking from the church and other common buildings. This will be used to build quarters inside the fort for the women and children. They will need my help with this, so I will be going to the fort today. I will expect that you will be packed and ready by tomorrow. I will come back to get you then."

Senōr de Cueva reached across the table and took his wife's hand. She was cradling a sleeping Benito with her other hand. When she looked up, their eyes met and held for a moment.

"Now honey," he turned to Luissa, "What do you want to know?"

Luissa stared at her father, opened her mouth then shut it. Her mind was filled with questions, but there were so many of them it was as if they were all getting tangled up with each other in her head. She couldn't sort them out enough to even ask a single question.

"We're all moving to the fort?" she asked in a quiet voice.

Her father smiled. "Yes. That sums it up, doesn't it?"

"Now, I have to gather my tools and take them to the fort to help with the construction of quarters." He got up from the table and went outside. Luissa's mother followed him outside, patting Luissa's shoulder on the way by, still holding her brother.

Luissa heard her parents talking in quiet voices out back. Although she was curious about what they may be talking about, she sat in a confused daze. She was trying to understand all that her father had just said.

The rest of the day was extremely busy for Luissa and her mother as they tried to organize the family's meager belongings. Warm clothes were a must for the cold weather. Not knowing what the living arrangements would be like inside the fort, blankets would be necessary. As far as valuables, the family Bible and other religious artifacts were the first to go into the small wooden chest that they would take with them. Some of the beautiful Timucua pottery, which would be practical as well, was carefully packed.

It was during this flurry of activity that Luissa's mind started to make sense of some of her many questions.

"How long do you think we will stay in the fort?" she asked.

"I really don't know," her mother answered. "But remember, the governor said to plan on it being an 'extended siege'."

"What does that mean?" asked Luissa. "Extended siege?"

"Extended means for a fairly long time and siege means an attack," explained her mother.

"More then a week?" she asked.

"Probably," said her mother.

"More than a month?" Luissa asked, her eyes getting wider.

"Maybe."

"More than a year!?" she practically shouted.

"No- I do not think it will take more than a year. Remember, the governor has sent for help from several areas. Other garrisons- Pensacola, Apalachee, Mobile. Even Havana. Once reinforcements arrive, I believe the siege will end quickly."

"Are those places far away?" Luissa asked.

"Yes, I would say that they are. Remember, not only do the dispatches for help have to get there, but then they have to prepare their soldiers and they have to get back here. That's why the governor says it may take awhile," Senõra de Cueva explained.

"What if they don't come?" asked Luissa. "Will we be stuck in the fort forever?"

"Oh Luissa," her mother smiled, "of course they will come. I assure you that we will not be living inside the Castillo de San Marcos forever."

Luissa folded another blanket then turned to her mother again.

"Have you ever been inside the Castillo?" she asked.

"No I haven't," her mother answered.

"Are you sure it is safe?" Luissa asked with suspicion.

Her mother laughed. "Luissa! The Castillo de San Marcos is the safest place in all of Spanish Florida!

Remember, it is built out of coquina. Coquina can resist any cannon fire. It took nearly 30 years to build that fort. That is why the governor is moving us inside the fort. We will all be safe from English attack."

Satisfied with that answer, Luissa turned her attention back to the storage chest. She carefully placed her rosary beads and the family crucifix beside the family bible. She froze as another thought came to her.

"Our house is not made out of coquina," she stated, turning to her mother. "Our house could get damaged in the battle."

"Yes, it could," her mother agreed. "But remember, it is just four walls and a roof. It is a thing, and things are not what are important. People are."

The next night Luissa was nearly sleeping when her father got home. She was lying on her moss-stuffed mattress next to the brasero, her dog curled up beside her. They were enjoying the warmth and glow of the coals while her mother rocked her brother to sleep. When she heard her father's footsteps, all sleep left Luissa's eyes as she jumped up to greet him.

"Papa!" she exclaimed as she threw her arms around him.

"My goodness, what a greeting! I was only gone for a day."

"Is the fort all ready? What is it like inside the Castillo de San Marcos? When are we going?" As usual, Luissa asked questions faster than anyone could answer them.

"We will go tomorrow," he said. "This morning more English ships were spotted sailing south, perhaps to block the passageway through Matanzas inlet. It cannot be postponed any longer."

All through the next day small groups of people made their way to the fort. Some families, like the de Cueva's, brought small trunks or canvas bags with them. Others brought nothing but the clothes on their backs. Some moved toward the fort in a rushed frenzy, while others strolled there as if on their way to a picnic. There were even some herding small groups of livestock into the dry moat that wrapped around the entire perimeter of the fort.

The only entrance to the fort was on the south side near the bay. The first wooded ramp ended at the ravelin, a small guard house. It was here that several soldiers were checking in the townspeople who entered the fort. The governor wanted to keep meticulous records so that any family turning in their food stores and livestock would eventually be compensated by the Spanish government.

After going through the ravelin, another wooded ramp led into the Castillo de San Marcos. This ramp was suspended over the moat and had a portion that actually retracted, acting as a drawbridge.

The process of checking people in was quick, but by afternoon, the number of families arriving at the fort increased so that the people of St. Augustine had to actually wait when they got to the entrance. The line of people grew each hour and by the time Luissa and her family arrived there were easily 100 people waiting to get in. When word spread that more English ships were spotted heading for St. Augustine inlet, the number of families waiting to get into the fort tripled.

"Luissa, please stop jumping around," pleaded her mother as they waited just outside the ravelin. They had been waiting in line for almost an hour and Luissa had not been able to stand still. There was so much to look at. She kept moving around to get a better look at the fort, the bay, even the other people in line. She had grown tired of that, but her tenseness prevented Luissa from settling down. She was feeling a confused mix of excitement and dread. To distract herself she knelt down and started scratching Lobo behind his scruffy ears. He seemed to be enjoying the attention, when he caught sight of a stray cat wandering among the trees across the street.

Immediately Lobo's body tensed, his ears twitched and his eyes narrowed in on his target. Before Luissa knew what had happened, he was off in pursuit of the cat.

As usual, Lobo ignored Luissa's calls to come back and both he and the cat disappeared into the woods.

Luissa stood and started to go after her dog when her father grabbed her arm.

"Papa," she cried, "we have to go get Lobo!"

"Luissa, you will never find him, you know that. He'll come back when he is ready. He always does."

"But papa," pleaded Luissa, "we are going inside the fort. Lobo won't be able to find us. When the English land, he won't know what is going on! What if they hurt him?" she stared at her father.

"Lobo is a smart dog. He takes very good care of himself and he will be fine," he tried to assure her.

Luissa's eyes filled with tears. "Papa please! We have to get him! We can't leave him out here with the English coming to attack! He will get hurt or killed!"

Luissa's mother put her arm around her daughter's shoulder as she cried. "Lobo will be just fine honey," She tried to soothe her. "His wild side will keep him safe, I'm sure of it."

Despite her parents' assertions that Lobo would be fine, Luissa was not so sure. Tears continued to stream down her face as she and her family made their way into the fort.

Chapter 5

On November tenth when the gates of the Castillo de San Marcos closed for the final time, there were more people inside the fort than the governor had anticipated. To his delight, the majority of the converted Indians had joined the Spanish in seeking the safety of the coquina walls of the fort. He had been afraid many of them would chose to leave the city and be killed by the English or the unconverted Indians helping them. Or worse- they would leave St. Augustine and the missions and return to their heathen ways.

Alongside the Indians and the Spanish inside the fort were an assortment of freed slaves and Mulattos. Including the soldiers already inside the fort, there were now over 1,500 people.

At the very center of the Castillo is a large, square, open courtyard. It was in this space that the temporary partitions and shelters had been constructed. Since the courtyard had no roof, small lean-tos had been built for protection from the winter rains that came this time of year. Three fresh water wells were in three corners of the courtyard. Every other available space was taken up by structures. Some were wooded; some made out of animal skin- any and all material had been used.

In the fourth corner of the courtyard was the huge ramp that went up to the gun deck that wrapped around the entire perimeter of the fort. At each corner of the gun deck was a diamond shaped bastion where lookouts were stationed. In the bastions, as well as scattered around the gun deck, were cannons, aimed and ready to defend the fort and the people inside.

On the lower level of the fort, surrounding the courtyard and under the gun deck, were various enclosed rooms. There were more than 15 of them and they each had a very specific purpose. There were artillery stores, storerooms for provisions, ammunition rooms, a small blacksmith shop, a jail, guardrooms, and even a chapel.

Luissa stood next to the tiny shelter that would now be home to her entire family and looked around the courtyard. She had never seen so many people in one place before. A great many of the faces she recognized, after all, she had lived her entire life in this garrison. Some she knew by name, others just from seeing them regularly about town. Some of the faces she studied as she looked around, she had never seen before.

She finally spotted Diego.

"Mama, there is Diego. May I go see him?"

Her mother was sitting on their small wooden chest, feeding her brother and her father was standing in the distance talking with a small group of men.

"I suppose so. But don't go anywhere else."

In a flash Luissa had made her way through the crowd to where Diego and his mother were trying to get settled.

"Well hello there Luissa," said Diego's mother, "I'm glad to see that your whole family got here safely."

"Not everyone-"she said, looking at her shoes. "Lobo ran off again and papa wouldn't let me go after him. He's somewhere out there." Her eyes were once again filling with tears as she looked up.

Diego looked at his friend. "Oh Luissa, he'll be alright. He's the smartest dog I know. He's as used to living in the wild as a real wolf. He knows how to take care of himself. You'll see."

"I hope you're right," she said, wiping the stray tear that had run down her cheek.

"Hey, did you hear about the ship?" asked Diego, changing the subject.

"The English ships?" Luissa asked.

"No-our ship."

"What about our ship?"

"We sank it," he stated emphatically.

"What do you mean- we sank it? Our own ship? That's crazy," Luissa said, shaking her head.

"It's true," said Diego. "Rodrigo got to come and say hello to us this morning. He is working as an artillery man in the southeast bastion. Papa is in the northwest bastion. Anyway, he told us the whole story. See- we had one of our frigates out in the inlet when those English ships- 13 of them I think- were spotted sailing into the inlet. The governor ordered the ship to sail into the harbor where it could be protected by the guns of the fort." Diego stopped to take a breath and went on.

"Because of the tides and the winds, they couldn't get the ship over the sand bar. They tried and tried and it just wasn't working. Well, those English ships were closing in so the governor ordered the captain to remove as many valuables as possible and to sink the boat." He finished his story and looked at Luissa.

"We sank our own ship?" she asked in disbelief. "That makes no sense. Why would we do that?"

"So the enemy wouldn't capture it," explained Diego.

"But now it's gone," Luissa said. "We don't have the ship anymore."

"But they don't have it either," said Diego with his hands on his hips. "This is a battle Luissa, you have to think like a soldier!"

Before the children could continue their conversation, a horn blasted to signal all soldiers to their posts for battle. Standing in the courtyard they could see the soldiers on the gun deck rushing around, making preparations and other soldiers- the ones not on duty- exiting from enclosed quarters and rushing up the massive ramp. It was clear that this was not a drill.

The first blast of the horn seemed to freeze the hundreds of people that crowed the courtyard. They all looked up at the activity on the gun deck. By the time the horn blasted for the third time, the huge crowd seemed to spring into action as well. Mothers gathered their children, families found each other and everyone retreated to whatever small space they had claimed as their own.

Luissa could hardly make her way back through the crowd of rushing people. She was halfway there when a strong arm reached through the mass and grabbed her wrist. Before she knew it her father was at her side, propelling her through the horde to her mother and brother.

Once together the family sat in their tiny space. Luissa sat on the ground and her mother was sitting on the trunk. Benito, in her mother's arms, had started wailing when the horns had first blasted, but was beginning to quiet down now that the horn had been silenced.

It was amazing to Luissa that so many people gathered in so small a space could be so quiet. A few muffled voices could be heard, mainly mothers trying to reassure their children. It seemed everyone was waiting. Waiting for something that would tell them exactly what was happening. People looked around, their eyes meeting each other's with questions.

Activity could be heard up on the gun deck, but since most of the activity was now on the exterior perimeter of the deck, those gathered in the courtyard could not get a clear look.

Luissa's mother and father were talking quietly together and then they hugged and her father turned to her.

"Luissa, I've got to go now. I want you to be a help to your mother with your brother."

"Where are you going?" she asked as she reached out and grabbed his hand.

"Not far," he smiled. "All of the Spanish men need to do their part to help in the defense of our city."

"But you are not a soldier!" she cried.

"You are right, but I am a carpenter. The governor needs my skills. I will be doing many things to help our soldiers and the people of St. Augustine while we are here. I may not see you very often." He quickly hugged Luissa and was across the courtyard, checking in with one of the soldiers on guard. Luissa saw the soldier point and her father entered one of the many small rooms that bordered the courtyard.

"The English must have landed," she heard one of the other women near them whisper.

Luissa looked around, straining to hear anything that would tell her what was happening. It was still fairly quiet, even though the people seemed to be relaxing a little bit.

At first, the low rumbling sounded like distant thunder to Luissa, but when it didn't stop, she knew it couldn't be that. The sound gradually grew louder as more people became aware of it and looked around in confusion. It was not only getting louder, but closer as well. Soon the ground beneath them actually shook with the vibrations. The thunderous sound rushed toward the fort and Luissa looked around in fear. She looked up on the gun deck. If this was the English army charging the fort, why weren't the soldiers shooting their guns and lighting cannons, she wondered. It didn't make any sense to her.

The roaring thunder continued until it reached the fort and seemed to actually surround it. It was then that the soldiers up on the gun deck burst into cheers and applause.

Luissa was totally confused. None of this made any sense to her! Almost immediately the gate to the fort opened and several Spanish soldiers rode in on horseback. They were smiling as they looked at the hundreds of bewildered faces that filled the courtyard.

"The English have landed, but we just herded 163 head of cattle through their lines and into our mote!" one of the soldiers cried.

A cheer went up from the crowd as Luissa looked at her mother. Her eyes were wide and she was sure everyone had gone mad. Cows? They were cheering for cows?

Senõra de Cueva tried to explain. "There is now going to be enough food to feed all of us if this battle goes on for a long time." she said.

Slowly Luissa nodded her understanding.

The jubilation of the people in the courtyard was cut short as the first cannon from the gun deck roared.

Almost immediately, the courtyard was once again quiet. It was obvious that the English had arrived in St. Augustine and were close enough to be within range of the soldiers' guns.

For several hours the cannons and guns roared. Sometimes the sounds were so close together that they blended together. Other times there were quiet lulls between the sounds of the cannon fire. Initially, the sounds made Luissa put her hands over her ears. It was a new sound to her and she hated it. But as the afternoon wore on, she got used to it. Luissa was actually surprised at how little the noise seemed to be upsetting her brother. Her mother had wrapped him in one of the blankets, carefully covering his ears to muffle the sound and he was sleeping soundly on the mat beside her mother.

It was then that Luissa heard it. A huge explosion. But this wasn't like the cannons being fired. Almost immediately all of the other gunfire stopped and she could hear running and shouting above them.

The people in the courtyard sat stunned. No one was sure what had happened or what needed to be done. Several soldiers yelled down for first-aid and other soldiers responded by rushing up the stairs with supplies.

For Luissa, what was actually less than half an hour, seemed like days. But soon an officer came down from the gun deck to address the crowd.

"One of our own cannons has exploded," he explained to the stunned masses. "It seems it was cracked and overloaded. It exploded. It killed three of our soldiers and injured five others."

A gasp went from the crowd.

"It was the cannon in our San Pablo Bastion. Our northwest lookout," the officer explained.

Luissa put her hand to her mouth as she nearly screamed. Her eyes wild, she looked at her mother, who was confused by Luissa's reaction.

"What is it Luissa?" she asked.

"That's the bastion where Diego's papa is stationed," she whispered in fear.

Chapter 6

Luissa and her mother, with Bentio in tow, were waiting with Diego and Senõra de las Alas for some word on Senõr de las Alas. Although no one said anything, Luissa hoped just being there would help. She wanted to say something to Diego. Something that would make him feel better, something encouraging and hopeful. But she couldn't put together a single sentence in her head that she thought didn't sound stupid. So she just sat there beside her very best friend.

He was looking into the distance, his eyes not focusing on anything. His face was expressionless, his body motionless except for his chest barely rising and falling with each breath he took.

Diego's mother was sitting with her hands folded in her lap, her eyes closed and her head bowed. Luissa's mother had placed one of her hands over Senõra de las Alas' hands and had her head bowed as well. The women were lost in silent prayer.

Luissa looked at them, then Diego and wondered what she should do.

It was then that Rodrigo appeared before them. He dropped to his knees and grabbed his mother's hands.

"He's alive Mama!" he said, watching the relief flood into his mother's face. "But he is wounded," he added.

"How badly?" she whispered.

"Pretty bad. He wasn't far from the cannon when it exploded. He got hit by quite a lot of flying, burning metal. Most of his wounds will eventually heal. But…" Rodrigo hesitated.

"But what?" said Diego, who had been sitting beside his mother since his brother had arrived.

Rodrigo took a deep breath, "His eyes were badly burned. The doctor thinks that the sight in one eye may come back, but the other eye was too badly damaged. He'll never see out of that eye again."

Rodrigo waited, allowing the magnitude of what he just said to sink in.

"But he will live!" His mother breathed, taking both her sons in her arms. "Thank the good Lord!"

"And you," Senõra de las Alas turned to Luissa and her mother, "Thank you for waiting and praying with us. You are dear friends."

With that, the de las Alas family went off to see with their own eyes that the Senõr was alive. He was being tended to, along with the four other wounded men, in one of the storage rooms. The governor knew that these would not be the last injuries, although he did hope that there would be no more disasters caused by their own equipment. He had one of the rooms turned into a hospital of sorts, stocked with what little first-aid supplies they had been able to scrounge up. It was in this small, dark, cold room that Diego's mother sat, holding her husband's hand through the night.

The next day dawned clear and cold, as Luissa and the other people in the courtyard began to stir. It was the second full day that they had been enclosed within the coquina walls of the fort and some of the details of managing 1,500 people within so small a space were just starting to get worked out.

Feeding everyone was the main concern. Most people of St. Augustine had brought their dried food supplies with them and had turned them in to the common storage room. But many of those seeking refuge in the fort- the freed slaves; converted Indians- were extremely poor and had nothing to donate to the common cause. The governor's advisors had even recommended that he turn away those who were not Spanish or were not from within the walls of the city. The governor had immediately refused to even consider turning away a single person who came seeking the safety of the fort. They would find a way, he believed.

So several times a day food was distributed to the crowds. Food was plain and meager, but no one complained. The governor had put in charge of this process, several soldiers who were too old to be able to help in the siege. Several others were stationed by the wells for security.

Diego had spent the night with the de Cueva family in their tiny space. His mother was determined to stay with her husband until his condition improved. It didn't take long for Luissa and Diego to become restless as the morning sun rose higher in the sky. Luissa's mother realized how difficult staying in one place was for children who loved to stay busy, so she sent them to fetch a pail of water from one of the wells.

As Diego and Luissa set off, they decided to go to the well that was the farthest away from them. That way they would get a better look around the fort. Making their way through the courtyard, they wove around small groups and families that were doing their best to settle in.

They were nearly to the well when they heard someone call their names. Looking around they spotted Junco and rushed over to where she was sitting with her family.

"Hello," they said in unison to Junco's parents and grandmother who were sitting on the ground. Her parents nodded their heads in greeting to the children who turned to Junco.

"I'm so glad you made it here!" Luissa exclaimed, hugging her friend. "Now you are all safe."

"Yes, we are here, but grandfather refused to come. He said this war is a sign that we must go back to old ways. He went with others of the Panther Clan. They went across the large river to where the sun goes down." She turned and glanced at her grandmother who was sitting very straight and staring down. Then she whispered, "Grandmother wanted to come with us, but now she is so sad, she doesn't talk or eat."

The children's conversation was interrupted by a quick blast from a horn. A Captain, halfway down the massive ramp got everyone's attention and then announced, "Governor Zuniga would like to address everyone. It seems there have been some developments of which you must be made aware." With that the governor exited the stone room that was now his

42

military office and climbed the ramp until he was sure that he was high enough for everyone to see and hear him. He stood silently for a moment, looking at the crowd, before he began.

"The English forces have arrived in St. Augustine from the west and now have control of the city. It seems they are using the friar of St. Francis as headquarters. Their ships have not yet landed, but since our guns will not be able to reach them, it is only a matter of time before they will join up with the troops already here."

He paused to allow what he had said to be absorbed.

"Our greatest obstacle right now is our own homes and buildings. They block our effective assault on their forces, and more importantly, our enemy can use the cover of these buildings to get close enough to the fort to do damage," the governor paused, and then went on emphatically.

"That is why we have no choice but to burn down any building within a musket shot of the fort."

A collective gasp went up from the crowd as they looked at the governor. Before anyone had time to voice a disagreement, he held up his hand to indicate quiet, and went on with his proclamation.

"I will be sending out a sally of soldiers and musketeers to set fire to the designated buildings. According to our maps, this zone will be anything 750 feet or closer to the fort, from St. George Street on the west to Cuna Street on the south."

Voices started to rise as the governor once again asked for quiet before he went on.

"The families affected will be able to- at their own risk I must stress- go and retrieve any possessions they may want to save."

With that, the governor purposefully marched down the staircase and back into his office.

Luissa's head was spinning. Her ears were ringing as the governor's words swam in her ears.

"The English have control." "We can't stop them." "Greatest obstacle." "No choice…" "Burn down buildings…." "Cuna Street." " Cuna Street."

Luissa dropped the bucket she was carrying and leaving both her friends standing stunned, she pushed her way back through the crowd to her mother.

By the time she got there, her father was already deep in conversation with her mother.

"Did you hear that?!?!" Luissa shouted in disbelief. "They can't do that!" she yelled. "They can't just decide to burn down someone's house!" Her voice rose in indignation. "They can't do that!" This time actually stamping her foot as she screamed. "You have to stop them!" she demanded, looking from one parent to the other.

She expected to see her parents' faces red with anger. She expected to see them as furious as she was. She expected that they would be ranting and pacing as they decided how they would save their home from being burnt to the ground.

What she didn't expect was to see them sitting calmly, their faces resigned to the fate that the governor had just bestowed on them.

"Luissa, come sit down," her mother patted the trunk next to her.

Luissa sat down in a huff. "What are you going to do?" she demanded.

"Nothing," her father said calmly.

"NOTHING?!" she shrieked, jumping to her feet again.

"Sit down Luissa," her father said sternly.

Luissa slowly sat back down and her mother took her hands in her own and looked into her eyes. She spoke very slowly as if she knew that Luissa would have a hard time understanding her.

"I know you are upset. But this is something that we have no control over at all. There is absolutely nothing we can do to change the facts."

As Luissa looked into her mother's eyes, she knew what she said was true. Luissa's anger seemed to evaporate, leaving in its place a helpless sinking feeling in the pit of her stomach.

"You mean they are really going to burn down our house?" she whispered, her eyes filling with tears.

Watching her mother nod her head, Luissa thought she was going to be sick.

Chapter 7

Luissa lay beneath several blankets in the cold night, staring up into the star-filled sky. She wondered how the stars could shine so brightly when it was such a dark night. Her heart felt black as she laid thinking over the last hours.

After the governor's proclamation, the fort had been frantic with activity. The families directly affected, those whose homes were within 750 feet of the fort, numbered more than 20. Most families, like Luissa's parents, understood the necessity of this drastic act although there were a few who tried to challenge the governor's orders. When they realized the futility of their arguments and the resolve of the military, they gave in as well.

Several of the families intended to leave the fort and try to rescue some of their belongings as the governor said they could. But Luissa's father had refused to even consider it, despite Luissa's pleas.

"Luissa, there is nothing in that house that is worth risking our safety to get." He was emphatic. Luissa couldn't think of anything to say to that.

So as she lay trying to fall asleep, all she kept thinking of was her house. She had been born in that house. It was the only home she had ever known. She thought about the small path that led off the street into the little courtyard. She remembered sitting in the shade of that courtyard many times while doing some of her chores- mending a torn skirt or grinding corn. She thought of the hanging shelf that was suspended over the table inside of the house. It was only recently that she had grown tall enough to reach it without help. Luissa thought about her father's shop in the backyard. She thought about all of the hours she had spent helping him- and sometimes not helping at all but just being there with him. In her mind she could see the small garden in the sunniest part of their small yard. In it grew the herbs that her mother used for cooking as well as medicines.

Luissa lay in the dark, tears silently streaming down her face and onto her blankets. It was going to be gone. The house. Papa's workshop. The garden. Everything.

When she finally drifted off to sleep, Luissa slept fitfully, tossing and turning. Her dreams were gray and dark and she was always lost. Searching and searching for home. She was alone and running, calling for her parents and her brother. Nothing about their town was the same in her dream. She just kept searching and searching.

When she finally woke up in the morning, the day was as gray and dreary as her mood.

It was another busy day in the fort as the main gate opened and closed several times to let people in and out. People who had decided to risk confrontation to retrieve some of their belongings. Soldiers were busy with their watches on the gun deck. Another group of soldiers armed and on horseback left the fort after meeting with the governor.

Luissa, Diego and Junco were sitting together, watching the activity at the fort gate from across the courtyard. Diego broke the silence.

"I bet they are bringing more letters asking for help," he stated.

"Why does he keep sending letters?" asked Luissa. "Isn't one enough?"

"What if the soldier carrying the letter is captured? The letter won't get through," Diego explained, "We would never know. The governor keeps sending letters just in case. Also, they may be taking different letters in different directions."

Luissa and Junco nodded their understanding as the children sat in silence once more.

This time it was Diego who didn't know what to say to his friend. He had never seen Luissa as upset as she had been since they heard the news yesterday about her house.

"Maybe help will come," Luissa said, "before we have to start burning down the houses." Her face brightened a little at the thought.

Diego wanted to let her believe anything that would make her feel better, so he just nodded, even though he thought that was an impossibility.

Junco looked at Luissa, started to open her mouth to say something, and then closed it again.

"What were you going to say?" Luissa asked her.

"I'm not sure how to say it…" she searched for the right words. "Your house will be gone, right?" she asked.

Luissa nodded.

"But you, your mama, papa and your brother safe, no?"

Again Luissa nodded.

"You brought your trunk with…" again she was searching for the right word.

"Yes, with some of our family valuables," Luissa explained.

"Well, why are you so sad?" Junco asked.

Luissa looked at Junco, shocked. How could her friend even have to ask such a thing?!

"Our house is going to be burned down," Luissa slowly stressed each word, thinking perhaps her Tumucuan friend didn't understand the meaning of the words.

"But your family will be alright? Yes?" she asked.

"Yes," Luissa nodded, "But our home will be gone."

"No-" Junco said, "Your house burned, yes, but your home is not gone."

Now Luissa looked confused. "If my house is burned down, my home is gone," she tried to explain.

"No-" Junco said again, "House- Home- not same thing."

"Yes they are," Luissa tried to explain to her friend. "House and home ARE the same thing."

Junco shook her head.

"House," Junco said, "is wall and roof," she used her hands to help show a roof. "Home," she said putting her hands on her heart "is here. And is everywhere the earth is." She extended her arms into a wide circle.

Luissa wasn't sure what her friend was trying to say.

When the evening dusk began to settle over the fort, a hushed seriousness settled in as well. The people knew that the governor was planning on sending out the sally of soldiers to set the buildings ablaze, after the sun had gone down. It was hoped that the cover of darkness would keep them safe from the English gunfire.

As the soldiers gathered at the gate, some with weapons, some with torches, they were silent. They knew the graveness of their mission. Some would even be setting fire to their own houses. They turned to look one last time at the hushed crowd before they swiftly left the Castillo de San Marcos.

Luissa was sitting on the blanket, hugging her knees.

"Mama," she asked quietly, "What if Lobo comes back to the house and it's gone?"

Her mother put her hand on Luissa's shoulder.

"Lobo is a very smart dog. He will stay safe until he finds us."

"What if I never see Lobo again?" Tears were once again streaming down her cheeks. Luissa felt like she had been doing nothing but crying lately. Before the siege, she used to think that girls who cried all the time were babies. She prided herself on being tough and strong, but lately she hated both those words. All she wanted to do was cry and cry and maybe kick and scream and pound her fists. Just like a baby having a temper tantrum. That's just what she wanted to do.

Her mother sat beside her on the ground and put her arm around Luissa's shoulders.

"Luissa, I know that this is the most awful thing that has ever happened to you," she said gently, "but I want you to remember that every single person in St. Augustine is going through this as well."

"But not everyone's house is getting burned down- by our own soldiers!" she whined.

"That's true," her mother agreed, "but this is touching every family in terrible ways. Just think of your friends. Diego's father may never see again. Junco's family has been torn apart. Every single person in the fort is being affected in some way. I don't want to scare you, but this siege is not over yet. We don't know what will happen tomorrow or the next day."

Luissa looked at her mother, fresh tears rolling down her cheeks. "What are we supposed to do then?"

"The most important thing is to have faith. To pray and to believe that things will work out. The second thing is to think about the good things that could happen instead of the bad things. Focusing on the bad 'what ifs', doesn't help at all."

It was then that Luissa and her mother noticed the night sky to the south and west start to glow. It glowed orange and yellow as flames started to shoot up in spires. Clouds of smoke rose in the sky and the smell of smoke began to permeate the fort.

Unlike the fires on Amelia Island the night the English had landed, these fires were close enough to hear and feel and smell. Although the high walls of the fort prevented them from having a clear view, they could hear the roar of the flames and the crackling of the wood as the blaze ate the buildings with fury. Soon, sparks even rose above the fort walls, glowing in the night sky until they rose far enough to cool and disappear.

No one slept that night as they all sat, each person lost in their own thoughts. Crowded into the courtyard of the fort, they were witnessing part of the city burning down around them.

Chapter 8

By morning the flames had subsided into pockets of burning embers, while the smell of smoke hung heavy in the air. The Spanish Garrison, having torched their own buildings, had burnt to the ground almost 30 homes. Only the soldiers on watch on the gundeck of the fort could actually see the ruin and rubble. The citizens gathered in the courtyard could only see the smoke still rising from several areas still burning.

Luissa, although she had tried to stay awake all night, had eventually been overtaken by physical and emotional exhaustion. She had fallen into such a deep sleep that even as others in the courtyard began to stir, she continued to sleep. The magnitude of what they had done to their own town hung heavy in the air, adding to a very subdued atmosphere in the courtyard. When Luissa finally did awaken, the sun was high overhead.

She had just finished folding her blanket when the gundeck came to life once again with the sound of gunfire. Without the houses to block their view and their aim, the Spanish soldiers were hoping to reach the English Army from the fort.

By late afternoon the gunfire seemed to have quieted slightly. Luissa asked if she could go see Diego and her mother gave her permission. As she wove her way through the crowd she heard bits and pieces of conversation. All were focused on their current situation. Some were speculating about the English Army. It's size and fire power. Others were guessing when help would arrive. Some conversations were even focused on plans to rebuild when the siege was over.

Luissa was lost in thought when she walked right past Diego.

"Hey Luissa!" Diego called, startling her. She came over and sat down with him.

"I thought my papa was the only one who couldn't see!" he joked.

"Diego!" Luissa was shocked. "How can you joke about a thing like that?"

"Luissa- it's alright. My papa is not going to be completely blind. He is getting his sight back in one eye. Even he jokes about it. He says if he can't be a soldier anymore, he'll be a pirate- he already has the eye patch! Sometimes joking about things make them seem less bad."

Luissa looked at her friend skeptically. "Some things are so bad you can't joke about them," she said emphatically.

Diego could see that she was talking about losing her house and he decided to change the subject.

For the next few days, life at the fort was predictable and started to settle into a routine. The older men would gather into small groups to talk, the women would tend to their children as best they could, and the youngsters began to forget the dire circumstances that surrounded them.

The passing out of the food rations twice a day also became the avenue for dispersing information. While waiting in lines, people gossiped and passed on information they had overheard or witnessed. The older militia men who were coordinating the entire process, gladly shared with everyone, any news or information they had heard.

It was during one of these morning sessions that Luissa and her mother heard that the English army and their governor, Moore, had set up camp on both the north and south sides of the fort. In the south they were using the St. Francis Monastery as headquarters; to the north they had taken over the Nombre de Dios Mission. Luissa reached out and took her mother's hand. Before the siege she used to think she was too old to hold hands with her parents while they walked through town. She thought that at 9 years old, she was very grown up. But lately, she felt more and more like a little girl. She even sometimes found herself wishing she were an even littler girl. Seeing her baby brother, so unaffected by the terrors that had been tormenting her, she thought how nice it would be to not understand what was going on.

Then she realized that even though she was aware of the events that were happening, she really didn't understand them. Sometimes just holding her mama's or papa's hand made her feel safer. Standing there now, the warmth of her mama's hand encompassing hers, she tried to understand what was happening to their town.

She tried to picture the English soldiers in control of St. Francis. In her mind she saw the chapel where they went on Sundays for mass. The ornate alter in the front in sharp contrast to the simple benches on which they sat. She tried to picture the English soldiers there and could not even imagine what they would look like. She heard they were taller than the Spanish soldiers. Were they gigantic, she wondered? Or perhaps just as tall as the Timucua Indians, who were also taller than the Spanish soldiers. Did they have evil faces?

She tried to picture them at the Nombre de Dios Mission. Were they in the rooms in which Junco and her family lived? The thought sent shivers up her spine. As horrible as losing her house was, Luissa realized that thinking about the enemy living and sleeping and using your home was almost as horrible.

As Luissa and her mother crept along with the crowd moving closer to the ration table, they also heard talk of the governor's pleas for help. Apparently two more messengers had been dispatched and were thought to have gotten through the English lines. With both the north and south sides of the city occupied, and the bay on the east, sending soldiers west was the most promising, even though it was a path of greater distance to reach another Spanish settlement.

"Do you think they got through Mama?" Luissa asked.

"Yes, I do Luissa," her mother replied, "Remember I told you that you have to have faith and hope. Without those two things, a situation like this would be unbearable. But with those two things," she paused for a moment, "I know we can endure anything."

Luissa nodded. She realized that she also believed that the messengers got through. She had to believe that because to believe otherwise would be unthinkable.

That was just what she told Diego later as they sat once again in an unobtrusive spot in the courtyard to watch and talk.

"I'm sure the messengers have gotten through," she said with authority. "The governor has sent so many."

"I'm sure too," agreed Diego.

Their daily conversations had become part of the routine of their nearly two weeks in the fort. They would share information they had heard. Sometimes helping each other understand what it meant; interpreting bits and pieces of conversation and gossip they had overheard. Many adults would engage in lengthy conversations, sharing information and facts, but no one thought it necessary to share information with the children.

"They just don't want us to worry," explained Diego when Luissa had complained about not being told things.

"But don't they know that we imagine the worst if they keep things from us?"

"Yes- that is true," agreed Diego. "In the first two days after my papa was hurt, mama did not want me to go to see him in the sick room. She was afraid it would upset me to see him like that. She said he needed his rest and that I would be restless just sitting there. Even though she told me he was going to be alright, I didn't believe her. I thought she wouldn't let me go see him because he was so bad he was going to die."

Luissa nodded. "I'm glad you finally got to see him."

"Look!" Luissa exclaimed, pointing to the southern sky in the distance. "That's smoke!"

"Where?" Diego moved and tried to look where she was pointing. "Are you sure that's smoke?" he asked.

"Sniff," she commanded, taking a deep breath herself. "I smell smoke. Something is definitely burning."

"That's the direction of the English army," Diego added. "Do you think they are building fires? You know, to stay warm?"

"That seems like an awful lot of smoke for a small fire. Look, it's getting thicker."

The children sat watching the smoke fill the sky. Being in the courtyard, all they could see was the smoke as it rose in the distance, so they continued to speculate on the cause.

"Oh no!" exclaimed Luissa as another thought came to her. "Do you think we are burning down more of our own buildings?"

Diego shook his head. "I haven't heard anything about that." He was as puzzled as Luissa.

It was only later that night when Luissa's father returned from the work he had been doing, that her questions got answered.

Senõr de Cueva had been up on the gundeck, adding reinforcements to the wooded platforms on which the cannons sat. With the constant use that the cannons now had, the platforms were not withstanding the impact of the slamming metal very well and were in need of repair already. The task had taken almost all day and that had been just one of the platforms.

Luissa knew that he must have had a good view from up there, so that was the first thing she asked him as he sat down.

"Yes, Luissa, it was smoke from fires that you saw today," he said wearily. "It seems that the English have burned down some of the buildings in the southern part of town."

"Why?" she asked, trying to understand.

"I really don't know," said her father.

Chapter 9

"I can't believe we have been in this fort for a whole month," said Diego as he and Luissa made their way over to one of the fresh water wells. It was still early in the morning, so the sun had not yet risen high enough in the sky to warm the courtyard of the Castillo de San Marcos. Over the last few days the weather had gotten even colder. Luissa, like many of the people in the fort, had put on all of the clothes that she had before going to sleep last night. The layered shirts, skirts and sweaters helped to keep her warm as she slept, but did make it difficult this morning to move easily.

They passed the bucket to the guard at the well who assisted them in getting their water ration. To protect the water supply from possible sabotage, the wells were always guarded or locked.

They had just hoisted the bucket out of the well and were starting back when there was a burst of activity at the fort gate that caught their attention.

A group of soldiers were raising their weapons while another opened the gate. In walked a man holding a gun above his head, a woman holding a baby and a little girl between them.

Luissa could see right away that they were not Spanish. They looked Indian, although she could not tell from which tribe they came. There was much commotion as the soldiers took the weapon from the man and continued to surround the visitors.

One soldier hurried away to the governor's quarters and in no time, was back. They then lead the family off.

Luissa and Diego couldn't see where they went and looked at each other puzzled.

"I wonder what that was about," Diego said as the children continued across the courtyard.

By the time the sun was high overhead it had warmed enough for Luissa to take off a few layers of clothing she wore, although the day was still cool. She and Diego, once again restless, had gotten permission to go find their friend Junco.

Because most Spanish families had brought some of their belongings with them when they came to the fort, they had stayed in one place in the courtyard. When they had arrived, most found a small space and settled into it, keeping their belongings close. However, the majority of the Indian families had nothing but the clothes they wore when they arrived. They had not found it necessary to settle in and claim space as their own. So they tended to migrate; one night sleeping in one spot, the next day perhaps a different space. Junco's family was like that, which made it more difficult for Luissa and Diego to find Junco. They had almost covered the entire courtyard before they found her.

"Junco!" Luissa laughed as she approached her friend. "We almost couldn't find you!"

Junco jumped up and stopped her friends from getting any closer. "You must go. Leave," she said quietly as she looked at her friends.

"Why?" asked Diego, puzzled, as Luissa looked beyond her friend to see what was behind her.

Sitting with Junco's family was the family that they had seen entering the fort earlier that morning. The man was deep in conversation with Junco's father. He was leaning very close so he could talk in a very quiet voice and Junco's father had a very serious look on his face. His eyebrows were furrowed and the corners of his mouth turned downward. The woman was holding both children and looking at the ground. Junco's mother was intently watching her husband's face.

"Hey, I saw them this morning," Luissa said quietly. "What's going on?"

"Please! You must go. Very important," Junco pleaded with her friends. "Please!" Her voice was quiet, but both her friends could see how upset she was. They had never seen her as agitated as she was now.

"But I want to know what is going on," explained Diego.

"I'll tell you later. Now you go. Now!" She motioned for them to go back from where they had come.

"Alright," they reluctantly agreed, "but come find us later," Diego added as they slowly turned and walked away, stealing glances back at the families.

Luissa, who was curious by nature, could hardly stand the suspense, and all afternoon speculated on the mystery.

"Maybe they are part of Junco's clan?" she guessed.

"Maybe," agreed Diego.

"But why wouldn't they be happier to see them?" she wondered.

"Don't know," answered Diego.

"Maybe they have news of Junco's grandfather?" Luissa guessed.

"Maybe," agreed Diego.

"But why wouldn't she want us to go near them?" she asked.

"Don't know," answered Diego.

"Maybe they are from another tribe and want to join their mission?" she guessed.

"Maybe," answered Diego.

"But what is so serious about that?" asked Luissa.

"Don't know," replied Diego.

"Maybe- "

"Luissa!" Diego interrupted, "You could guess all afternoon with your 'maybes' and it's not going to make any difference. All we can do is wait for Junco to be ready to tell us. You know I'm right."

"Maybe," smiled Luissa.

Diego laughed.

"You know that I like to know what is going on and things with no answers drive me crazy!"

Later that evening while they were eating their supper rations, something else happened that added to the mystery. After evening rations were dispersed, most people sat down on the ground or on blankets to eat so the view around the courtyard was unobstructed. Luissa was sitting on the trunk with her mother and baby brother. Diego had taken his rations and had gone with his mother to visit his father.

From where she sat, Luissa could see the governor on the gundeck at the top of the ramp talking to several soldiers. They were scanning the crowd below, obviously looking for someone. When they finally spotted who they were looking for, the soldiers rushed down and charged through the crowd. Luissa sat with her mouth open, watching the excitement.

The soldiers grabbed the Indian family who had entered the fort that morning. The soldiers were very rough with them, especially with the man. He kept talking to them and trying to shake free of their grip, but the soldiers never said a word and simply dragged the family into one of the rooms that was being used as a jail. The governor and several of his captains followed them into the room and the door was slammed shut.

The crowd in the courtyard sat in stunned silence. Everyone seemed as puzzled as Luissa.

The next morning, more questions surfaced as she and Diego sat eating their rations. He could hardly wait to tell Luissa what had happened the night before.

"...so we were just sitting, eating supper with papa in the hospital room. He can sit up now and walk around even- with some help," he was saying. "Anyway, all of a sudden we started hearing these screams and yells from the next room! They stopped, then came again. It was so awful!" He took a mouthful of grits, and then looked at Luissa. "All kinds of noise and stuff."

She stopped eating and her eyes grew wide. "Hey- I think the hospital room is right next to the room where they took that Indian family last night!" Then she explained to Diego the peculiar happenings that she witnessed the night before.

"Wow!" he said. "That is strange."

It wasn't until several hours later that all of the strange events of the last two days fit together and made sense. Junco had the missing pieces of information and when she finally sat down with her friends, they were anxious to hear what she knew.

"Who were those people with your family yesterday?" asked Luissa, getting right to the point as usual.

"The man is Juan Lorenzo, a Yamasee Indian. He and his family are bad. Very bad," she said shaking her head.

"What do you mean? What did they do?" asked Diego.

"They come to fort making like friend. Ask for protection and give-" Junco was searching for the right word, "tell what he know about English Army."

"Oh, information!" Luissa added. "He was volunteering to give information about the English, right?"

Junco nodded. "Yes, so he tells what he knows and governor says he can stay in fort."

Luissa and Diego looked at each other then at Junco. There had to be more to the story. This certainly did not explain much.

"After he was free in fort," Junco went on, "he started finding other Indians- Yamasee, Guale,

Apalachee- and tell them to fight the Spanish," she looked at her friends to see if they understood what she was trying to say. Although her command of their language was adequate, sometimes she struggled to express exactly what she wanted to say.

"He wanted Indians to battle inside fort to help English," she clarified.

Luissa's eyes grew huge as she started to understand. "You mean to actually turn against us?"

Junco nodded.

Diego, his expression serious as he listened, shook his head. "But that makes no sense. The Indians don't have any weapons. There is no way they could overthrow our soldiers. They would never win."

"But that's not-" Junco again struggled to explain. "They were not trying to win. They just wanted to cause...mix up...confuse soldiers."

"They just wanted to cause a commotion here in the fort?" Luissa was trying to understand what Junco was trying to say.

"Yes," nodded Junco.

"But why?" asked Diego.

"Then Juan Lorenzo plan to sneak into powder room and blow it up," she said.

This time Diego's eyes grew wide. "Oh no!" he gasped.

"Papa went to soldiers to tell them," explained Junco, "Before bad things happen."

"Your papa turned them in?" asked Diego, obviously impressed.

"So soldiers could capture him before bad things happen," she added.

"They must have been questioning him in the room last night," said Diego, putting together the last puzzle pieces.

Luissa, who had been sitting quietly for the last few minutes, suddenly sat up straight.

"The powder room has all the ammunition, right?" she asked. "The gun powder, cannon balls, bullets, everything?"

"Yes," Diego agreed, "if they destroy that, our soldiers wouldn't have been able to keep fighting the English."

"You don't understand Diego," Luissa said, "If he blew up the powder room with all of that gun powder and stuff in there, we all might have been killed, at least a lot of us." She motioned to the crowded courtyard of people.

The three children sat in silence as the magnitude of what might have happened engulfed them.

Chapter 10

In the days that followed the attempted Indian assault, the weather grew increasingly colder and damp. The winds off the water blew enough moisture into the air to cause the temperature to seem even colder. The frigid dampness penetrated even the thickest layers of clothing.

The governor decided to allow several fires to be built in the courtyard, in hopes that the warmth would permeate the crowds and perhaps stay trapped within the high coquina walls. This did help to ward off some of the coldest temperatures until a day of torrential rain. The driving rain not only put out the fires, but also soaked all of the St. Augustine citizens thoroughly.

When the rain finally subsided to a mere drizzle, the fires were restocked. Unfortunately firewood, like all of the supplies in the fort, was limited, so only a couple of hearths were relit.

Luissa and her family were too far from either fire to enjoy any of the warmth. Luissa's mother had her take off her outer layers of clothing and wrap herself in one of the blankets. Luissa sat shivering in the afternoon grayness while her mother wrapped her brother in the other blanket. Finally, as evening wore on, Luissa and her brother began to warm up.

It was then that Luissa noticed her mother's clothes were still wet and she was shivering.

"Mama, you are freezing. Share my blanket."

"Not now honey," she said. "You need to stay nice and warm."

That night Luissa was roused several times as she slept by the sound of her mother coughing. She could tell that her mother was trying to muffle the sound so as not to wake up her and her brother. When morning came Luissa could see that her mother had gotten very little sleep. It was the first time since the siege began that her mother looked haggard and discouraged. She wasn't her normal cheerful self. Even with all of the setbacks of this situation, her mother was always the one to stay focused on the positive. Luissa knew that she must be upset and worried, but she never let it show. This morning, with the exhaustion and the aches and pains she was feeling, she wasn't even making an attempt to be cheerful.

Thankfully, the day dawned clear. Although it was still cold, there was no sign of rain, so everyone hoped that the strong sun would help to dry out some of the dampness that still lingered from the day before.

After morning rations, which Luissa noticed her mother only picking at, she offered to play with Benito so her mother could rest.

"Oh honey," said her mother, "That's very sweet, but he is still only four months old and a big responsibility."

"Well, I am 9 years old and a very responsible girl," she stated emphatically. "I can do it."

Her mother looked at her standing there with her feet apart and hands on her hips and smiled.

"Yes," she said, "I believe you can."

Luissa quickly picked up her brother.

"Now wait a minute!" Her mother smiled. "You can take care of him in this general area while I rest. You aren't going off anywhere and I'll be right here if you need me. Alright?"

"Alright," she agreed.

Her mother had barely laid down when she drifted off to sleep. Even this sleep was broken by occasional fits of coughing, but Senõra de Cueva didn't even try to quiet her coughs now that it was daytime and the courtyard was busy with activity and noise. Soon the coughing died down and she settled into a deeper sleep.

Benito was a happy baby and now that he was four months old, he smiled and laughed all the time. His favorite thing to smile at was his big sister Luissa, who made the funniest faces and the silliest noises.

Luissa was busy making those funny faces and entertaining her brother when Diego came up behind her.

"Is your Mama sick?" he asked quietly when he saw her mother sleeping.

"Oh Diego, you startled me," said Luissa. "Yes," she explained, "Mama is sick from the rain and cold. I'm taking care of Benito."

Diego joined Luissa in making silly faces and sounds and soon they had Benito laughing, that low belly laugh that babies do, which made Luissa and Diego laugh as well.

"What a happy trio!" Luissa's Papa said. "That is music to my ears." He smiled, then looked at Luissa's mother sleeping.

Luissa quickly explained about her mother's cold, and then asked her father what he was doing here in the middle of the day.

"Seems the English have been busy building gabions and trenches closer to the fort and moving their artillery up. They have been constructing them on the south and west for days now," he explained. "Those were bad enough, but now it seems they have a row along the north side of the fort." Knowing that the children wouldn't understand the significance of this latest development, he went on to explain. "That is the side of the fort that the marshes are on, where we go to cut grasses for the cattle in the mote to eat."

"Oh," said Diego.

This was one of the jobs that Luissa's father had undertaken since they had retreated into the Castillo. While his main trade was that of a carpenter and his skills were invaluable during the siege, the work they had for him did not take all of his time each day. Not one to sit around when things needed to be done, he had volunteered for some of the tedious tasks that anyone could do. This helped to free up the limited trained soldiers they had for the important task of defending the fort against the English.

"What are we going to do?" Diego asked.

"A sally of soldiers and others are going to go out and try to destroy as many of their gabions as possible," he stated, then went on in a serious voice, "I am going with the soldiers. The governor wants the gabions to the north destroyed first and since I know those marshes so well, I am going along to help." He looked at Luissa to see if she understood.

She simply stared back. She was afraid to say anything. She was sure if she opened her mouth to say anything that she would start crying and she knew she couldn't do that. Instead she just nodded and picked up her baby brother.

"When are you going?" asked a hoarse voice from behind them. It was only then that they realized that Senõra de Cueva was awake and had heard the conversation. She looked at her husband.

"This afternoon," he stated. They said nothing more, but simply looked at each other. Luissa knew that they were definitely communicating. She knew from years of experience that her parents had some kind of special language- a language of looks or a touch- that said so much without either one of them saying a word.

Senõr de Cueva then got up, kissed his wife and Luissa and then was off before anyone could say anything else.

The rest of the afternoon, no matter what Luissa and her mother were doing, they were listening intently for the sounds of artillery, which would indicate a confrontation outside the fort.

It had been 5 weeks now since they had taken refuge in the fort and everyone had grown accustomed to the intermittent exchange of gunfire between the English soldiers who controlled the city and the Spanish soldiers on the gundeck. The battles were sporadic. Sometimes they would last for entire days, sometimes for a few hours, and sometimes they would go a whole day with no exchange of gunfire at all.

The English had discovered that the coquina walls of the fort were indeed impenetrable. The coquina was porous and easily absorbed the force of bullets and even cannonballs without cracking or crumbling. It was then that Governor Moore had decided that the only way for his forces to conquer the fort would be to get close enough for the cannons and artillery to clear the high walls of the fort and land inside the courtyard.

Governor Zuniga knew how disastrous that would be, so despite the risks of sending men outside the fort, he knew he had to in order to destroy the English trenches and gabions.

News of the 58 men leaving the fort and their mission soon spread through the entire courtyard, so once again the atmosphere was subdued and serious. Some people had gathered in small groups to pray, while others simply sat listening for any sounds that would indicate what was going on outside the Castillo de San Marcos.

Luissa was sitting lost in thought. She wished she could stop thinking, because her mind was once again playing the "what if" game on her. What if they don't destroy the gabions? What if the English do get artillery into the courtyard? What if one of those bullets hits her brother? Or her mother? What if her father is hurt while outside there fighting? Or worse?

Luissa remembered what her mother had said about staying focused on the positive. She decided to try the "what ifs" looking only at the good things that could happen. What if the men did destroy the gabions? What if they all came back unhurt? What if help finally arrived and chased the English out of St. Augustine? What if they finally got to leave this fort and go home?

Home. She remembered then that their house was gone. Then she remembered what her papa had said. People are more important than things. She knew that he was right and if he came back unhurt, and her mother and brother did not get hurt, that even if they had no house when this was over, it would be alright.

It was then that her thoughts were interrupted by the cannons on the gun deck roaring to life. Those blasts were loud, but in between they could hear the distant exchange of gunfire that was the Spanish sally to the north of the fort coming face to face with the English forces.

The battle seemed to go on for hours and the waiting seemed unbearable. This time Diego and his mother were the ones offering support to Luissa and her mother as they waited through the endless afternoon.

For awhile the gunfire died down to an occasional blast and the cannons would be quiet for some time. Then they would all roar to life again as another confrontation ensued.

The gates to the fort finally opened as the sun started to set and the men rushed in. Some were wounded, some carried items that they had taken from the English trenches, and a few of the soldiers carried men who were obviously seriously wounded. Those men were taken to the hospital room while the captain of the group reported to the Governor on the outcome of the attack.

When Luissa finally saw her father making his way across the crowded courtyard relief flooded through her. He was dirty and exhausted, but didn't look wounded as she ran to him and threw her arms around him.

After reassuring herself that he was alright, she asked him a question that had been on her mind all afternoon.

"Did you see Lobo Papa? Remember, those marshes used to be his favorite place."

"No honey, I didn't see Lobo," he said gently, putting his arm around her shoulders.

Later that evening, before he had to report back to the soldiers quarters, he sat with all of them and shared what had happened.

The Spanish sally did force the English to retreat and were able to destroy most of the northern line of gabions and had even taken some tools and supplies that had been stashed in the trenches. Then the English had regrouped with some soldiers from the Nombre de Dios Mission and had charged the Spanish again. There was one soldier killed and several wounded.

"And the worst part," Senõr de Cueva was saying, "is that the English are already building new trenches less than a musket shot from the Castillo."

"So we didn't win this one?" Diego asked.

"No one did actually," Luissa's father said, and deciding to be completely honest added, "But it doesn't look good for us at all. Our only hope at this time is for help to arrive from the other Spanish outposts." He looked at Diego and Luissa, then at the two women.

"The governor had ordered 12 soldiers- 10 infantry men and 2 corporals- to leave tonight to get help. They are rounding up the fastest horses we have," he stated.

"So all we can do is wait?" asked Luissa in a discouraged voice.

"No," said Senõra de Cueva, her voice still hoarse from the cold and coughing. "There is something else we can do. We can pray." With that she took Luissa's hand and Diego's, who took his mother's hand. They all bowed their heads, praying silently and feverishly that the soldiers would be successful in getting help. They all knew that this was their only hope.

Chapter 11

Luissa sat holding her baby brother in one arm while the other she had placed on her mother's back. Her mother was overcome by another fit of coughing and Luissa could see that the wracking coughs were painful. She remembered the few times she had been sick, that the touch of her mother's hand, while not making her better, had provided much needed comfort; a cool hand on a feverish forehead or a protective pat on the back. Luissa was hoping that she could, in some small way, make her mother feel better.

Senõra de Cueva's cold had gotten steadily worse over the last couple of days. The hoarseness caused by coughing had settled into heaviness in her chest that caused her to have an almost constant shortness of breath. The sporadic fits of coughing were so intense that her ribs ached from the force of them. She was alternately getting chills and fevers at night. She tried to continue on as if she was fine, but it soon became obvious that even the most routine tasks were taxing her meager strength.

Luissa had taken over the care of her little brother. At first her mother had protested, but then realizing that she truly did not have the strength, she gave in. While Luissa's mother still fed Benito, Luissa had taken over the chores of changing, dressing and entertaining her brother.

Luissa also continued to fetch the daily bucket of water used for drinking and washing for the entire family. It was on these daily treks across the courtyard that she would find herself yearning for the open spaces of St. Augustine; the fields where she would run and play with Diego and Junco and some of the other children in town, the stretch of sand along the bay where she would wade in the water with Lobo and throw him a stick to catch, her own backyard, the town square.

Luissa was an active girl and the inactivity of being confined within the Castillo de San Marcos was beginning to bother her. She could not take a step in any direction without coming face to face with someone. With all of the people of St. Augustine in the fort, personal space and privacy was a luxury they could not afford. The space for children to run and play was no where to be found. At times Luissa felt that her legs actually ached from the desire to break into a run or a skip.

Luissa was not the only one who was beginning to find the length of the siege discouraging. The morale of everyone was taking a beating. As she wove her way through the crowd to the well, she saw fewer smiles, heard less laughter and even noticed that the conversations- groups of people talking together- were rare.

Knowing that the English forces had not only taken over their town, but had surrounded the fort so completely, had been a setback for everyone. Despite the governor's pleas for help, they had heard nothing. For the first time, the possibility of defeat seemed likely.

Luissa was grateful that Benito was too little to understand their situation. His smiles and laughter not only cheered her up and gave her something to focus on, but also helped her to believe that everything was going to be alright. Luissa was playing with her brother when Diego came and sat beside her.

"I see your mama fell asleep," Diego said quietly. "She's still not better?"

"No. And there are no more medicines here so I don't know what can make her better," said Luissa. "Where have you been?" she asked.

"I went with mama to see papa. He is well enough now to be up and about. He still needs to walk with a cane because his leg has not healed right, and he wears a patch over his bad eye, but he is alright," he explained with a smile.

"That's good," said Luissa, then hesitating she asked, "Diego, what do you think is going to happen?"

"You mean with the siege?"

Luissa nodded.

"Well," he began slowly, "I want to believe that some Spanish soldiers are going to arrive to help us win this battle."

"But what if they don't come? I mean, how is this going to end if we don't get any help?" She looked pointedly at her friend.

"Eventually we would have to surrender," he stated quietly. "We do not have enough food or ammunition for this to go on much longer."

Luissa nodded her agreement as she played with her brother.

"What happens when- I mean IF we have to give up?" she asked her friend.

"That's a good question," he agreed, "I'm not real sure. I guess the English then have St. Augustine. It won't be our home anymore."

"What happens to us?" Luissa looked up in surprise. This was the first time she had thought through the possible consequences. "Will we be prisoners?"

"I really don't know," admitted Diego. "I imagine for awhile. Then we'd probably have to leave."

"Leave?!" exclaimed Luissa. "Leave and go where? St Augustine is our home."

"Luissa," Diego said, "I really don't know any more than you do. I'm just taking guesses. But think about it- if we lose, St. Augustine will not be our home anymore. It will belong to the English."

Luissa could not fathom the thought of St. Augustine not being her home. Her mind raced with scenarios and questions. None of the scenes that played themselves out in her head were pleasant. In fact, most of them were so discouraging; she turned back to her brother.

"I don't want to talk about this stuff anymore," she stated emphatically.

That surprised Diego since Luissa always wanted to talk and always had a long list of questions. But he respected her wishes and neither of them talked about their precarious position for the next couple of days.

December twenty-fourth dawned cold. Luissa's mother was not the only one sick. As the cold and dampness settled into the Castillo de San Marcos, many people were catching colds. Because of the cramped quarters and lack of hygiene, these colds spread very easily.

The ill health that some were experiencing only served to add to the feelings of defeat. Even the soldiers seemed to have lost their resolve, as they went about their tasks in a much slower manner, almost as if the possibility of losing were an actual weight around their neck.

As Luissa waited at the well to get her bucket filled, she couldn't help overhearing two old women talking as they waited as well.

"It is no use," said one. "Even if help should arrive, the English have sent for help too. When their reinforcements arrive, we will surely be defeated."

"Yes," nodded the other. "I think we should just surrender now before we suffer an attack that is likely to get many of us wounded or killed."

"What is the governor thinking?" the first woman added as they got their bucket and started off.

Luissa was in a daze, her mind going over the conversation she had just heard. Was it really that hopeless, she wondered?

"Feliz Navidad!" said a happy voice behind her, as Luissa turned to see Diego.

"What?" she asked.

"I said, 'Feliz Navidad.' Don't you know what day this is?" he asked. "Today is Christmas Eve. Tonight is the celebration of the birth of Christ," he said.

"It can't be," said Luissa in disbelief. "We've been in here since the beginning of November. Are you sure about that?"

Diego nodded. "Yes. The priest is making plans for a special mass tonight."

Luissa could not believe it. In some ways it felt like she had been inside the fort forever, yet in so many other ways it seemed like just yesterday when she and Diego were picking berries with Lobo in the thicket outside of town. The day the governor had first spoken in the town plaza. The day it had all begun.

Diego and Luissa were walking back with the bucket when a yell went up on the gundeck. It caught the attention of everyone in the courtyard as one of the lookouts blew his horn. They watched as the governor rushed from his quarters and up the huge ramp. The hush in the courtyard was tense as everyone silently wondered what was happening.

Several minutes passed before the governor came back into sight at the top of the ramp. Everyone watched and waited.

"Two ships have been spotted out on the horizon," he stated as a gasp went up from the crowd. "They are still too far out at sea to determine if they are English or Spanish ships. I will let you know when we have identified them." With that he disappeared back into the depths of the gundeck.

Everyone looked around to see if they had understood what the governor had said. Two ships? They could be Spanish! Or they could be English. They could finally have the help they needed to win back control of their city. Or they could suffer the final blow and lose the battle.

For the next several hours people tried to go about the day normally, but they all knew this was not a normal day. People were tense and worried. Some gathered in prayer in small groups. Some sat in silence, lost in their own thoughts.

Luissa and Diego tried to play with Benito, but they could hardly concentrate. Neither of them knew what to say, so no one mentioned the ships or the possible outcome of this event.

The sun was high overhead when the governor returned to the edge of the gundeck. As soon as he stood there, it was as if everyone in the courtyard knew he was there. Conversations ended, prayers were finished and everyone turned to look expectantly at their leader.

The winter sun was so bright that it caused many to squint, but even with the glare it was clear by the governor's stance and expression that the news was not good.

"I'm afraid the ships are English," he stated in a steady voice.

A cry of despair went up from the crowd. Almost immediately sounds of weeping could be heard from across the courtyard. Some collapsed in grief, others started to feel panic grip them, and still others- like Luissa- simply stood frozen in a state of shock.

Chapter 12

Luissa walked the courtyard carrying Benito, as much to comfort herself as to calm him. In the hours since the governor had announced that the ships on the horizon were English, Benito seemed to sense that their situation had taken a turn for the worse and his normally cheerful disposition had turned whiney and impatient. Luissa's mother was still feeling quite ill, so was trying to rest again. Benito wanted no part of their usual silly games, which gave Luissa no choice but to try to distract him by walking.

He had started out wiggly and unhappy, but soon became interested in the sights and sounds around them. Luissa, on the other hand, had grown less aware of her surroundings as time went on and was now so lost in thought that she was totally unaware of her environment.

"Luissa!" called a friendly voice.

Luissa looked up, startled to see Junco.

"You going somewhere?" asked Junco.

"Not really," replied Luissa, "I'm just kind of walking to distract Benito. He was grumpy."

"I'll walk too?" asked Junco as she fell into step beside Luissa.

It hardly seemed possible, but the mood in the fort had gotten even worse. Most people felt that this latest event was the beginning of the end for them. They had tried to go about things as normally as they could, but for many, they had lost all hope.

"Look!' whispered Junco, pointing to the ramp. There at the top stood Governor Zuniga, waiting for the attention of the masses. It didn't take long for everyone to quiet down, as they were anxious to hear what he might have to say.

"As you are aware, tonight is Christmas Eve. I think that in honor of this holy day we should have a celebration." The governor paused as people looked around in confusion.

"I will be giving orders that extra food and drink be distributed, we will have music, I shall even be giving a bonus to the soldiers."

The people in the courtyard, as well as the soldiers, continued to stand in silence. Most were not sure how to react. The governor sensed this.

"I know how discouraged everyone is feeling, but we must not give in to despair." His voice was like steel as he continued.

"Our determination is our greatest weapon. We will not lose this battle if we continue to have faith. Faith that our comrades will come to our assistance. Faith in ourselves that we will endure and prevail. Faith that we will have the strength to save our city." The governor paused for his words to reach out to everyone. "We will not lose this battle. We will not lose our home."

The silence hung in the air. Everyone wanted to believe him. They wanted to believe that despite the current circumstances, they would win this battle.

Slowly, in a far corner of the fort, someone started clapping. Soon the clapping spread across the Castillo de San Marcos.

The governor stood looking down at the crowd, his very stance conveying his determination. His steadfast belief that he and his soldiers would be able to prevail seemed to radiate from him.

Many in the crowd felt that if the governor was this determined and sure of himself and his troops, how could they doubt? They wanted and needed to believe that things would work out and the governor stood there giving them a reason to hold on to hope.

Luissa and Junco looked at each other. Slowly a smile crept onto Luissa's face.

"Maybe we can win this," she said to her friend.

That night the fort was filled with festivities. The governor had instructed that several huge bonfires be built and these flames not only filled the courtyard with light, but created enough warmth to chase most of the winter chill from the area. Any soldier not on watch had joined his family, which increased the crowd and the feeling of celebration.

Luissa was delighted to have her father with them. Since taking refuge in the fort, she had missed her father tremendously. Even though he tried to check in regularly with the family, it was different than life before the siege when he worked right in their backyard and Luissa could see him anytime.

Even Senõra de Cueva had perked up and said that she was feeling a little better. She still looked pale and had sporadic fits of coughing, but she was sitting with her family, holding the baby and smiling.

Luissa wanted to take this feeling and keep it forever. Her whole family was together and happy, just like before. Even Diego's family was together this evening since both Rodrigo and Senõr de las Alas had joined them.

For the first time in days, the courtyard was filled with conversation and happy voices. People were not only feeling hopeful, but were thankful as well. Thankful for their loved ones and feeling optimistic about the future.

As the evening wore on, the celebration only grew more festive and rambunctious. Soon a small group of soldiers started singing and encouraging others to join in with them. By the time they finished their song nearly everyone was singing along. Someone started another song, this one a Spanish dance song. Soon the crowd was united as they sang together; some even joined arms and began to dance.

The party lasted nearly all night and Luissa sang along on any songs she knew at the top of her voice. It was well after midnight before her mother and brother both fell asleep, yet Luissa continued to sing along and even occasionally, to dance. She grabbed her father's hand and even coaxed him into joining her for some of the dances.

"Oh Luissa," he laughed when he finally sat down. "You have worn me out."

"You're not done papa!" she cried in disbelief, "The party's not over."

"Maybe not for you," he grinned, "but an old man like me can't sing and dance the whole night. I have to sit for awhile."

"Oh, alright," Luissa sat down to catch her own breath. It was nearly dawn. The bonfires had dwindled to a couple of small fires and many of the crowd had succumbed to exhaustion and were sleeping. A few pockets of people still singing and dancing remained, but even their festivities were more subdued.

Luissa's eyes were getting heavy and she leaned against her papa sitting next to her. The next thing she knew it was morning and she was laying on her blanket, another blanket wrapped around her. Her mother was feeding Benito. She sat up and looked around.

"Well good morning sleepy head," smiled her mother. "You must have been up all night. It is almost the middle of the day."

"Where's papa?" Luissa yawned and stretched, trying to wake herself up.

"He's back to work. But he will be joining us when we have our Christmas Day Mass."

Luissa looked around the courtyard and could see that she was not the only one getting off to a slow start. The courtyard was quieter than normal and people seemed less active.

"Do you want me to go fetch water?" she asked as she folded her blankets.

"Diego brought me some this morning. He said you looked like you needed sleep," her mother explained. "He is a very good friend."

Luissa didn't have a chance to thank Diego for his thoughtfulness until they had all gathered that afternoon for their Christmas Day Mass.

It was a very solemn service. The festive atmosphere of the night before had faded and in the stark brightness of the winter day, it was impossible to ignore their dire situation. The English had gotten reinforcements and they had not. The people of St. Augustine knew that they were safe for the time being. It was this that they focused on as they celebrated the birth of their Lord.

Chapter 13

"Well I think it was the stupidest thing in the whole world!" said Diego emphatically.

Luissa looked at her friend in surprise. "Why?" she asked with a frown.

"Because it didn't change anything," he said. "It was like everyone was pretending it was going to be alright, but they knew it wasn't. How can people be so dumb?" he asked with disgust.

They were talking about the Christmas Eve celebration. Luissa was bouncing Benito on her lap as she sat with Diego and Junco. After the Christmas mass of the day before, her mother's cold had gotten worse. Her coughing had lasted almost the entire night and had exhausted her. After feeding Benito this morning she had fallen asleep, so Luissa had once again taken over the care of her brother.

"Well I think it was a good thing to do!" Luissa said stubbornly. "People were feeling so bad. The celebration helped them to feel better," she explained.

"Sure they felt better. But it was only for a little while. Now everyone feels bad again," he countered.

Diego was right. The atmosphere was as bad as it was before, perhaps worse. People were sullen and discouraged. The governor's determination was unshaken, but he was having trouble getting the soldiers to believe that they would prevail.

There was also the feeling of dread as people waited to see what impact the new English ships would have on the siege. After the Christmas mass of the day before, word came that the ships had anchored at Anastasia Island and had brought more arms and ammunition for the English forces.

"But I don't understand," argued Luissa, "What is so bad about feeling good for just a little while? Just forgetting about the siege?"

"Because," yelled Diego, jumping to his feet, "some people can't forget! Like my papa! He walks with a cane now and can't see out of one eye. It's hard to forget that." Diego's face had started to turn red as he continued to yell. "Maybe it's easy to forget if nothing bad has happened to you, but I can't forget!" he finished in a huff.

Luissa's eyes flashed with an anger that Diego didn't expect. "What do you mean if nothing bad has happened to you?!" She demanded, her voice getting louder. "My house got burned down by our own soldiers, you dope! That's bad! And Lobo is gone! That's bad!" She was yelling now and her eyes shone with tears. "Bad stuff has happened to all of us. And just for a little while it was nice to try and forget all of that." The tears were spilling down her cheeks as she finished. "Even if it didn't change anything."

Diego stood there looking at his friend, as she looked down at her baby brother. Junco looked from one to the other, than shook her head.

"You're all funny. You expect battles should bring good things? You're mad and surprised when bad things come? Battles always bring bad things," Junco tried to explain. "Indians know, even honorable battles bring bad things."

As the day wore on, Luissa became more and more concerned about her mother. Senõra de Cueva's fever seemed to be getting worse and when she did drift off, it was a fitful sleep. Despite the cold afternoon, beads of perspiration formed on her forehead and neck and when she talked, she did not make any sense. This final symptom scared Luissa more than the others. It was almost like when the old man down the street got so sick. He would sit in the chair in the front of his house, making sporadic gestures and ranting and raving about nonsense. Luissa's mother said he was harmless, but Luissa had crossed the street to pass his house. Then as quickly as he got sick, he died.

Luissa had gone to get Diego's mother. She was hoping that she would be able to get some herbs from the hospital room and they could make a tea out of them. Perhaps that would help her mama.

But as they both sat beside Luissa's mother now, Senõra de las Alas shook her head. "There are no more herbs left," she said.

"She is really sick, isn't she?" asked Luissa. "We have to do something. She doesn't know who I am."

"Yes," said Diego's mother gently, taking Luissa's hand. "We will do something. I need you to first get me a piece of clothe that I can tear up. Then I need you to fetch a bucket of water for me."

By the time Luissa got back with the water, Senõra de las Alas had torn the cloth into strips. She dipped them into the cool water and then began to lay them across Luissa's mother's forehead and neck.

"We must help cool her to bring the fever down," she explained. "Whenever she wakes enough, we must get her to have some sips of water. She is becoming dehydrated."

"What does that mean?" a horrified Luissa asked.

The Senõra smiled. "It just means that she is not getting enough water into her body."

"Oh," said Luissa.

For the next couple of hours, Luissa helped Senõra de las Alas to try to cool her mother down. The cool clothes that they put on her soon became warm from her feverish skin, so they would re-dip them in the cool water and reapply them. They were also able to get several sips of water passed her parched lips.

After a while, Senõra de las Alas was summoned back to the hospital room where she had been helping with some of the wounded soldiers.

"I can do it now," Luissa assured her.

"Alright," she smiled. "I will be back if you need me."

Luissa continued tirelessly with the routine. Soon she was dipping the cloths and applying them so automatically that she did not notice all the time that passed.

"Luissa," said her mother in a tired voice, "Where is Benito?"

Startled, Luissa grinned at her mother. "You know who I am!"

"Of course I do," she said as she struggled to sit up. "What is all this?" She pointed to the strips of cloth piled next to her.

Luissa explained to her mother about her high fever, Senõra de las Alas' help and that Junco and Diego were playing with Benito.

"My, I must have given you quite a scare," said her mother, putting her hand on her own forehead. "I think my fever might have broken."

Leaning back against the chest, it was clear her mother still did not have her strength back, but she was smiling brightly. "You are quite a big help my Luissa! Quite a big help!"

It was then that one of the lookouts in the bastion sounded the alarm. More ships were spotted in the distance. Again, tenseness descended on the fort. Would these ships be English? Would they be bringing more ammunition and even more soldiers? Would this be the final blow to the Castillo de San Marcos and all of the people inside?

Or would the ships be Spanish? It was almost too much to hope for. Once again the people of St. Augustine bowed their heads in prayer as they waited.

The wait seemed endless, but finally the governor addressed the crowd.

"We cannot be certain yet, but the four ships in the distance appear to be Spanish!"

The crowd gasped in delight.

"I believe they are the relief fleet from Havana. In order to be absolutely sure, it is imperative that there be quiet in the fort. The guards will be attempting to communicate with the ships and we must be able to listen and watch- to see if in fact, these are Spanish ships."

With that order given, the governor disappeared on the gun deck.

The crowd in the courtyard was completely silent. They all knew how important it was and they all wanted to do their part.

Luissa, Diego and Junco were sitting with Luissa's mother while she fed Benito. Luckily, the hours that Diego and Junco spent playing with Benito seemed to have tired him out and he was drifting off to sleep.

Looking around the courtyard, Luissa noticed that even the small children seemed to understand how important it was to be quiet. It was astonishing that this many people could be this silent. In the silence, Luissa strained to hear something- anything. She could hear the faint lap of the waves in the bay against the shore. She could hear the caw of birds and the sound of the cattle in the moat. It amazed her that in this silence she could hear so much. But no sound related to a ship. As time wore on, people continued to hope and to pray.

When it was finally determined that the ships were in fact, Spanish, a great burst of cheering erupted from the courtyard. A fleet of Spanish ships had answered their pleas for help! People hugged and cheered and laughed and cried. Many fell to their knees in prayers of thanks.

When night came to the fort, the atmosphere inside was one of rejuvenated hope. The soldiers were now as determined as the governor, that they would prevail. The people were openly hoping that with the reinforcements on these ships, they would be able to secure a quick victory and leave the fort to return to their homes.

As Luissa lay trying to fall asleep that night, she was once again struggling with mixed emotions. She was so very happy that help had arrived. With the end of the siege now in sight, her thoughts were on their return home. Their house, however, was gone.

The next morning the stirring of activity in the courtyard seemed to start even earlier than normal. People were now excited about what the day would bring instead of dreading the disasters of each new day. They didn't have to wait long for more good news.

Before the sun had cleared the gun deck, word came that it appeared the English ships in the harbor were making preparations to leave.

Chapter 14

"I sure wish I knew what was going on out there," mumbled Luissa, more to herself than to her companion.

She and Junco were sitting in the far corner of the courtyard. The December day was freezing, yet the sun was bright and blinding. The girls were each bundled in several layers of clothing, yet the cold from the ground still penetrated, causing them to shiver and periodically shift positions.

They had chosen this spot in hopes that they could catch a glimpse of the activity going on up on the gun deck. With the arrival of the Spanish ships the entire direction of the siege had shifted. Until then, the English had the upper hand and the advantage. However, after more than 6 long weeks, they had still not been able to defeat the Spanish. Now the possibility of an English victory seemed much slimmer.

While everyone in the fort was now optimistic that the Spanish would eventually prevail, they knew the siege was not yet over. There were still many English soldiers stationed throughout the town of St. Augustine, some still surrounding the fort. They also still had several ships in the harbor.

After the rumors that the English ships seemed to be preparing to leave the bay, no other information came, although the activity on the gun deck seemed to increase. Luissa and Junco hoped to get some idea of what was going on as they sat watching the soldiers and officers move about overhead.

"Will more guns fire?" asked Junco.

"I don't know," answered Luissa. "I supposed there might be. I can't imagine that after all this the English would just leave."

"I very much do not like guns," said Junco.

"I know what you mean," agreed Luissa.

"Hey, guess what?!" said Diego breathlessly as he came charging up to the girls. "I've been looking everywhere for you two."

"We've been right here," said Luissa. "Where have you been?"

"I was with my brother. Rodrigo told me what was happening." Diego was obviously agitated and anxious to share what he knew as he flopped down on the ground next to his friends. He looked at the girls and grinned as he sat there.

"Well??" Luissa said exasperated. "Are you going to tell us?"

Diego laughed at Luissa's impatience. "Well, the English ships are turning around and getting ready to sail out of the bay. They know that those four ships are Spanish and that if they don't get out of the bay, when the Spanish sail into the bay, they will be trapped."

"Alright," said Luissa, "But we kind of knew that."

"Well, did you know," Diego said emphatically, "That the governor is trying to contact the Spanish ships because they have anchored out in the sea? He wants them to actually charge into the bay and trap the English ships. They will have an honest to goodness ship to ship battle!" He actually sounded delighted at the prospect.

"Why are you so excited about that?" demanded Luissa in an accusatory tone.

"Because," Diego sounded surprised, "I want the English to get what's coming to them."

"I just want them to leave," countered Luissa. Then as a second thought she asked, "Are the Spanish ships sailing in?"

"That's the problem," explained Diego, "Rodrigo said that the governor is angry because the Spanish ships are just sitting there."

"They aren't going to help us?" cried Luissa.

"Of course they are," Diego said, "but they might not want to do it in the same way that the governor wants."

"Oh," she said, then asked, "Who's in charge?"

Diego paused. "Don't know," he stated as they all pondered the implications. "The governor, I thought. But I guess the captain of the ships is in charge of the fleet."

As the sun set that evening, word spread through the crowd that the Spanish ships were indeed starting to sail toward the bay. While they were still quite a distance out to sea, it looked like they would be able to prevent the English ships from fleeing.

It was difficult for Luissa to sleep that night. She lay looking at the stars in the clear, cold night, her mind racing with possibilities. Her restlessness was shared by most of the people in the fort. They could feel that the end of the siege was in sight. But despite their optimism, no one was sure how things would end.

By noon the next day, they started to get some answers, as a lookout was shouting observations that were being relayed to the governor. The people close enough to hear quickly told others who also passed on the information. People were anxious for some word on how the battle was progressing, so word spread rapidly through the crowd.

The English ships were turning around! It seemed they knew they could not get out into open sea before the Spanish fleet closed in on them, so they gave up hope of outrunning them. Instead, they were sailing back into the inlet. The infantrymen on the gundeck then began an assault, firing cannons in hopes of hitting the ships as they sailed back.

For Luissa, the sound of the cannon, which used to make her cringe, actually sounded hopeful and victorious now. So mesmerized was she by the activity, that she was surprised to see the sun actually begin to set behind the fort's west wall.

"Is it evening already mama?" she asked her mother, who for the first time in days, was getting color back in her cheeks. She was still tired and weak, but the fever had not returned and even the cough had eased.

""Yes indeed! Time is passing quickly for you now?" her mother smiled.

"Oh yes," agreed Luissa. It was amazing to her that this afternoon had passed so quickly when so many other afternoons during the siege had dragged by so slowly.

By the time nightfall came again, the cannons were once more silent and Luissa again lay looking up at a clear, star filled sky. As she lay on her back she started to notice the puffs of smoke slowly drift into the cold air. She followed the trail of smoke with her eyes and though she could not see the source because of the fort's high walls, she thought she saw flickers of light. Sitting up she took a sniff. There it was- the undeniable smell of something burning.

"Mama!" Luissa whispered urgently into the dark. "Something's burning!"

"I believe you might be right," her mother agreed.

"What is it?" she wanted to know.

"I have no idea," her mother said slowly.

It wasn't until several hours later, when her father returned, that Luissa got some answers. Her father explained that when the English were unable to escape the bay, they landed their ships, unloaded artillery and soldiers, and set their ships on fire.

"Why would they do that?" exclaimed Luissa.

"So that their enemy could not capture and use their ships," her father explained.

Luissa just shook her head in disbelief. "This is just crazy. They attack us, so we sink our own ship and burn our own houses, then help for us comes so they burn their own ships. I just don't understand."

Senõr de Cueva patted his daughter on her shoulder. "When it comes to battles, not very many things do make sense."

During the next 24 hours so much happened so quickly that it was difficult for Luissa to keep it all straight in her mind.

As the day dawned, the English ships were nearly completely destroyed by the fires, and the English soldiers were organizing themselves to march across land to safety to the north.

The soldiers on the gun deck were on constant lookout now. They tried to keep track of the moves of the English troops, as well as the Spanish ships that had sailed to the southern passageway out of Matanzas Bay and had anchored there. The soldiers on the deck were dispatching their observations to the governor, who was intently trying to plan the best moves to attain victory.

Just as the sun set, there were cries and shouts from the gundeck. Soldiers rushed to their posts and guns and cannons roared to life.

In the courtyard, Luissa and Diego had been finishing their evening rations. They looked around in confusion. The others in the courtyard looked equally confused. Soon someone pointed to the sky in the distance. Thick clouds of black smoke billowed into the sky.

Several hours later word came. The English troops were indeed leaving St. Augustine on foot and were marching north to meet with other contingents on their way back to Carolina. As they left St. Augustine they were torching everything. Every home, building, church and barn was being set on fire.

Luissa, like everyone else, sat horrified as the night wore on. Soon the night sky was bright in all directions as flames grew and spread. Smoke filled the air and cannon and gunfire from the fort never let up, in hopes of slowing some of the destruction.

No one slept that night. Luissa sat holding her mother's hand. She wasn't sure if it was the thick smoke or the absolute horror of what was happening that was causing the tears to stream down her face.

Chapter 15

December thirtieth dawned cold and dark. Even after the sun had risen, the sky was still gray. Thick smoke filled the sky and blocked out any possible sunshine. The gunfire from the deck had slowed through the predawn hours as the English troops, in retreat, had gotten farther and farther from the fort. Now, as the morning wore on and visibility increased slightly, the lookouts had gotten word to the governor that there were no more enemy soldiers in sight.

It was then that the governor dispatched a group of soldiers to leave the fort and scour the town. Before he opened the gates of the Castillo de San Marcos, he wanted to be sure that there were no pockets of soldiers waiting to assault them. Although the governor knew that the damage was going to be extensive, he also knew that casualties had been minimal and he wanted to keep it that way.

The people of St. Augustine continued to keep vigil in the courtyard as they waited. Although everyone knew that the siege was over, there was no joy or jubilation. Instead, there was an almost eerie quietness as many still sat in shock, trying to absorb the reality of the night's events.

Luissa's mind was racing. She sat in silence, staring at nothing, her mind a jumble of thoughts and emotions. She was happy, and scared, and angry and sad and confused all at the same time. Her stomach was doing somersaults and questions kept popping into her head. But for once, Luissa didn't ask any of the questions. It was as if she were afraid of what the answers night be and asking them would make them real. So she continued to sit in silence, while her mother tended Benito beside her.

When the governor finally issued the order to open the gates of the fort, the courtyard burst into a flurry of activity. Families gathered what meager belongings they had, and then everyone bowed their heads as one of the priests led them in a prayer of thanks. Then the gates were flung open for the first time in 51 days and the people of St. Augustine streamed out of the fort.

Luissa descended the ramp of the fort, tightly holding her father's hand. She gasped in horror. The town of St. Augustine, as far as she could see in every direction, was a mass of destruction. There were no buildings left standing. Instead, there were piles of debris and rubble where buildings used to be.

As they slowly made their way through the streets, Luissa could hear cries of disbelief and the weeping of despair as people wound their way through their beloved town. Everything was so familiar, yet nothing was the same. The charred remains of some homes still smoldered as thin streams of smoke rose toward the sky. The smell of burnt wood hung so thick in the air, Luissa though it would make her sick.

As they approached their street, the de Cueva family's steps slowed and they hesitated. Her mother, holding Benito, reached out and took her father's hand. Luissa, still holding his other hand, tightened her grip as they started down the street.

There, where their house used to be, lay a pile of ashes. One wall partially stood, but was charred so severely, it looked as if it would crumble if touched. Even though Luissa had known her house would be gone, the reality of seeing the destruction was a shock.

Senõra de Cueve found a tree stump and sat down with Benito on her lap. She was still weak from being sick and the walk from the fort had been exhausting. Luissa's father began to pick his way through the rubble to see if anything could be salvaged.

Luissa couldn't bear to watch so she turned to face the woods. It was then that she noticed the movement. Coming along the path of trees in the distance was a creature, limping so severely that each step was painfully slow. Luissa sucked in her breath as she tried to focus on the animal. She knew instantly that it was her beloved Lobo and she let out a scream as she ran to him.

He was thin and covered in dirt. His front leg was crusty with dried blood and he winced in pain every time he put weight on it. His fur was matted and Luissa threw her arms around him as she dropped to her knees in front of him. Although Lobo was extremely weak, he licked Luissa's face and his tail thumped the ground slowly. Luissa just sat hugging her dog as tears streamed down her face.

As she and Lobo made their way back to her parents, Luissa could see that he was struggling with each step. Lobo laid down slowly next to her mother and Luissa's father knelt down to look at the dog's injuries.

"He got himself roughed up pretty badly. Looks like he got shot in the leg, but the bullet went right through."

"Oh no!" wailed Luissa.

"It's alright," her father assured her. "He'll be fine. He's just going to need some time to heal." Senõr de Cueva looked at his family and added, "I think we're all going to need time to heal."

Luissa sighed and looked at the remains of her family's house. "Our home is gone," she said.

"Oh no," her father said seriously as he took her chin in his hand and looked into her eyes. "We saved our home. St. Augustine is still ours."

Glossary of Historic Terms

Apprentice- a person under a legal agreement to work for a length of time for a master craftsman in return for training and instruction in that trade.

Artillery- firearms and ammunition typically used by the military

Barter- to trade for goods and services instead of using money

Bastion- a projecting part of a fortification, usually at the corners

Brasero- large metal pans filled with hot coals and used to heat homes

Coquina- a natural limestone composed of crushed shells compressed over thousands of years. Mined out of the ground, it was used to construct buildings like the Castillo de San Marcos.

Frigates- a square-rigged warship

Gabions- trenches dug into the ground to allow soldiers to get closer to the structure being attacked

Garrison Town- a town whose existence is due to military presence.

Missions- a place run by a church and used to teach and convert others to their religious beliefs

Musket- a heavy, large-caliber shoulder firearm

Mulattoes- a person of mixed-race parents

Plaza- a public square in the center of town, used as a market and place to get and receive information.

Ravelin- a guard house, stationed as the first stop into a fortified structure like the Castillo de San Marcos

Sally- a rushing attack by troops of a place under siege

Sentry- a guard or lookout

Siege- an attack by an enemy trying to take control of a place

Tradesmen- a person who works in a trade or craft

Historical Timeline of Actual Events in the 1702 Siege of St. Augustine

October 27, 1702- Governor Jose de Zuniga y Cerda gets word that the English forces are planning to attack St. Augustine. He sends for help, informs the people of St. Augustine and readies the soldiers.

October 28, 1702- The Governor orders all soldiers to the fort and gives orders that no one in St. Augustine is to leave the city walls without permission.

November 3, 1702- The English, lead by Governor Moore, land on Amelia Island north of St. Augustine and burn the Spanish Missions there.

November 4, 1702- Governor Zuniga issues an order that all men over the age of 14 are to report to the fort to be armed and put on duty.

November 6, 1702- Governor Zuniga, receiving word that English ships have been spotted and troops are approaching by land as well, orders all 1,500 people of St. Augustine into the Castillo de San Marcos for protection.

November 9, 1702- The Spanish sink their own ship when it gets stuck on a sand bar in Matanzas Bay and they are unable to get away from the approaching English soldiers.

November 10, 1702- A cannon in the northwest bastion of the fort explodes due to a crack in it. The explosion kills 3 soldiers and injures 5 others.

November 11, 1702- Governor Zuniga orders that all homes and buildings within cannon fire of the fort be burned down so the English cannot use them as cover.

December 14, 1702- Juan Lorenzo, a Yamasee Indian, and his family come into the fort for safety. It is discovered that he was trying to sabotage the Spanish position by setting fire to the powder room where the ammunition is stored.

December 19, 1702- Spanish soldiers leave the fort to destroy English gabions surrounding the fort. They have some success.

December 24, 1702- A lookout spots two ships on the horizon. They turn out to be English ships. The people of St. Augustine are devastated and begin to lose hope. The Governor orders a holiday celebration to cheer everyone up.

December 26, 1702- Four ships are spotted out in the ocean. They turn out to be Spanish ships. The people of St. Augustine are hopeful that this will mean victory for them.

December 27, 1702- The English ships try to sail out of Matanzas Bay but are blocked. They are forced to turn back, unload soldiers and arms and set fire to their own ship.

December 29, 1702-The English retreat from St. Augustine, leaving by land heading north. As they leave they set fire to every building in St. Augustine.

December 30, 1702- The gates of the Castillo de San Marcos open and the people of St. Augustine leave after 51 days. They find a city completely destroyed, but still Spanish.